Adèle Geras
silent snow, secret snow

YOUNG PICADOR

First published 1998 by the Penguin Group

This edition published 2003 by Young Picador
an imprint of Pan Macmillan Ltd
Pan Macmillan, 20 New Wharf Road, London N1 9RR
Basingstoke and Oxford
www.panmacmillan.com

Associated companies throughout the world

ISBN 0 330 41500 X

3 5 7 9 8 6 4 2

A CIP catalogue record for this book is available from
the British Library.

Typeset by Intype Libra Ltd
Printed and bound in Great Britain by Mackays of Chatham plc, Kent

For Jonathan Appleton

it hides us
spirals down
never falling
falling is hard   it hurts
blown smoke-white from a black sky
it clings to everything
covers it   a comfort to the heart
masking what we know

silent snow secret snow

From *The White Room* by C. G.

This is how you get there. Leave the motorway (and remember it may be dark. It's wintertime). For about five miles the road is well lit, but later it winds and twists up into the hills. There's sloping woodland on one side of the car and a drop into blackness on the other. Follow the road down into the valley. It unwinds along level ground for miles, but still it curves and bends and you begin to think: I'm going back the way I came, but you aren't. The hedges are high on both sides of the road. Soon you'll get to the village. There's a pub and a church, a few small cottages and then you'll come to a tall, wrought-iron gate. You can see something through the metal curlicues: a shadowy mass rising into the night sky. There's a light in almost every window though, beckoning the visitor. Welcome!

Standing beside the bonfire on Guy Fawkes' Night, Laurie Springer turned to his friend, Carlo Masters, and said: 'Come and spend Christmas with us at my grandmother's.' His face was half-shadow and half-flame.

Carlo smiled and said: 'Sure, why not? That'd be great.'

Over the next few weeks, Laurie prepared Carlo carefully for the visit. The first task was to teach him who was who in the family. Irene Golden, Laurie's grandmother, owned a hotel: the Golden House. Her three daughters would all be there at Christmas: Letta (Laurie's mother), Susanna and Carrie, and then there was Susanna's daughter Ellie, short for Elvira.

Of course, Carlo had already met Marianne, Laurie's sister, and his father, Derek, was the History teacher at the boys' school. Poor old Laurie! One of the main reasons Carlo became his friend was because he felt sorry for him. What a disaster – being taught by your own dad! Carlo couldn't even imagine *having* a dad, much less what it would be like if he stood at a desk and pronounced on Disraeli or whatever in front of the whole class.

'I am', he told Laurie the first time they'd spoken, 'part of a one-parent family. My one parent is called Bette. Pronounced "bet". She was christened Betty with a "y", but she reckons Bette is classier.'

What he didn't tell Laurie was that he had once been Carl. Ages and ages ago. He'd practically forgotten all about it, because he was definitely more of a Carlo. The name suited him: the sort of person he wanted to be.

'I should tell you', said Laurie, 'about the Work Rota.'

'What's that?'

'Irene puts up a list of duties . . . washing up, hoovering, et cetera. The normal hotel staff who live mostly in the village don't come in over Christmas, so everyone has to help. And of course we all clean our own rooms and make the bed and so on.'

'I do that anyway,' Carlo said. 'And I'm a dab hand with a dishcloth.'

'I'm more of a duster man, myself. It's OK, actually, with

two or three people working together. It doesn't feel like work. Not really. More like fun.'

'I can't wait,' said Carlo.

'And I forgot to tell you the rule about presents,' Laurie said. 'Children in my family aren't allowed to buy presents. We can make them if we like. Irene says this is only right and proper in such a large family. There are thousands of us.'

'Thousands?' Carlo smiled.

'You know what I mean. There'll be eleven of us this year, if you count Nana and the Maestro.'

'You've lost me,' Carlo sighed. 'I've worked out most things, but you've never mentioned Nana, and who or what is the Maestro?'

'Nana is . . . well, everything really. She cooks and looks after everyone. She used to be the nanny when my mum was small. She's the housekeeper, I suppose. She's ancient.

'And the Maestro's real name is Frederick. He used to be a pianist centuries ago. Then he became a conductor. Now, poor chap, he's just the Madman in the Garret. I thought every household had one.'

'Not my household. There's only me and Bette.'

'Won't she mind you not being home over Christmas?'

'I shouldn't think,' said Carlo, 'she'll even notice. She'll be impressed. She'll say: "Christmas in a posh hotel? You've landed in the jam, you have." I don't think she'll realize that the hotel is closed over Christmas. She will ask me if I have any decent underwear. "I don't want you showing me up" will be her very words.'

Laurie laughed. 'And have you?'

3

'Nothing but the best for me,' said Carlo. 'Go on about the presents. You're allowed to get them, are you?'

'Sure. Grown-ups have money. That's what Irene says.'

'But you're nearly seventeen. When do you stop being a child?'

'We stop when Irene says we can,' Laurie said.

Carlo smiled. 'She's the boss, eh?'

'And how,' said Laurie. 'Only Queen might be a better word. Or even Empress. Yeah, definitely. Empress.'

Just before Christmas, Bette found a brochure for the Golden House pushed inside a magazine at 'Tresses', the hairdresser's where she worked as a receptionist. She called it a 'salon', and Carlo understood very well her desire to give things grander names than they deserved. He did that too. It was, he thought, depressing evidence that he *was* Bette's son and not the magical, glamorous changeling he had always longed to be.

Finding the brochure: that was a good omen, a lucky sign. It was printed on thick, cream paper and, in Carlo's opinion, it was a thing of beauty. He took it carefully out of its safe hiding place between the pages of his school atlas, and read it for the thousandth time . . .

The Golden House

is a private hotel set in wooded countryside near the village of Wedderling. The house was built in the Gothic style by Sir James Wedderly in 1835, and the gardens were landscaped by William Naismith.

Today, the Golden House provides a luxurious home away from home for the discerning guest who relishes peace, beauty and every conceivable comfort. There are fifteen bedrooms (each with en-suite bathroom) and the hotel is a television-free zone. There is a well-furnished Library, a Music Room and a south-facing Conservatory.

The Golden House is renowned for the quality of its vegetarian cuisine.

Those who are allergic to cats should be warned that the lovely, long-haired Pamina is a much-loved member of the family.

The Golden House is closed to the public between 15 December and 15 January.

Telephone and fax: 019890–325 468

He looked at the ten small parcels lying on his bed, and then put them into his rucksack. He was ready. He tried not to see the bed itself, nor the rest of the furnishings. Soon, he said to himself. Soon, I'll be gone. I'll leave this beige, predictable room and this beige, predictable life behind for a while.

'Discoveries await me,' he said aloud to his reflection in the tiny mirror stuck over the sink. 'I shall take these offerings to the inhabitants of a foreign land.'

Because, he told himself, that's what it is. A country with its own Princess. Carlo allowed himself to consider Marianne. This usually made him feel faint, so he didn't do it very often. It was a little like opening a box and looking at a priceless jewel that no one knew he possessed. All this was in his mind. He'd barely spoken to her, but now he was going to be in her company for four days. There were times when he felt like pinching himself to make sure he wasn't dreaming.

He could hear Bette and The Latest downstairs, giggling, and then she called up to him: 'When are they coming to fetch you, Carl petal? It's time we were off.'

'Any minute now, Mum,' he said, muttering 'Carlo, Carlo,' between gritted teeth. 'You can go now. I'll come down and say goodbye.'

He picked up his rucksack by one strap and glanced briefly over his shoulder. This isn't me, he thought. I need a better room, another life; one that glitters round the edges. I belong somewhere else. Not here. I belong somewhere beautiful.

22 DECEMBER

While the family made its way to the Golden House, the snow started to fall. At first it was only a few flakes swept off the windscreen by the ticking sweep of the wipers. Nothing to worry about.

5.00 p.m. The Garret Room

Irene, Nana and Carrie were too busy getting everything ready to notice the snow, but up in the Garret Room someone was watching the white crystals spiral down from the sky. Frederick Sternblatt used to be, once upon a time, feared and loved in every Opera House in Europe, but nowadays he looked like a frail and pale old man, with wispy white hair and long, skinny fingers like a skeleton's. His eyes watered and so, if he wasn't careful, did his nose.

Long ago, he'd been madly in love with Irene Golden. She married rich Ivor Golden instead of him, and has felt a little guilty ever since. That's why, the Maestro thinks, she lets me live here in this garret, and why she looks after me so well. Never mind . . . I'm happy. I am a little confused sometimes, but I know that I am happy.

The Maestro has been known to stand at his window for hours. He says the view soothes him. When Carrie asked him once why he'd chosen to live at the top of the house instead of down in the basement near Nana, he'd answered: 'It's a terrible thing not to be able to look out of the window. Terrible.'

Now, the garden spread out below him and the trees and shrubs looked like miniatures because he was so high up. He could see the Lake and the spire of the church. And the sky! Oh, how he adored the sky! Now, he'd been rewarded for this adoration by the sight of the snow falling. Glorious snow! Snow blotted everything out. Snow made its own strange light in the darkness. He watched the first flakes landing on the sill outside his window, and smiled with pleasure.

7.00 p.m. The Front Hall

Irene didn't look like a grandmother. Her clothes were wrong. They were more like costumes you might see on the stage than normal, everyday gear – long, robe-like things made of velour or satin, in dark reds or deep blues. Her hair was grey, but it was piled on top of her head, inter-twined and elaborate, and some people even believed it was a wig. It wasn't.

She insisted on being called by her real name and 'Granny' was a term she refused to recognize. She knew all about luxury. She understood about soft things and silky things and lovely fragrances and carpets your feet could sink into. She had a talent for colours and the way things ought to look, and how to put plump cushions in all the right places. She also had a horror of the cold, which meant that the Golden House, even when the world outside was frozen into white, was always deliciously warm.

She stood on the doorstep to welcome them all, and the yellow light behind her spread over the drive.

'Come in,' she said. 'Come in . . . you must be Carlo, darling.'

Laurie winced. In a moment, she would turn her attention to him and call him 'Laurence'. She always did. Why, he wondered, were families so toe-curlingly embarrassing? All the lessons he'd given Carlo had been a waste of time. Introducing your nearest and dearest to friends was utterly cringe-making and that was that. Laurie looked at his Aunt Susanna, at that moment shaking Carlo by the hand. She was looking frightful. Why? He hadn't seen her for weeks and it seemed to him she'd shrunk and grown greyish all over. And why was she having such trouble smiling?

'Hello!' Ellie's face, Laurie noticed, lit up when she saw Carlo. Well, he had that effect on most people. During the drive, Laurie had paid special attention to Marianne to see how she would behave. She'd been very cool and distant, but that didn't mean much. She was, Laurie knew, very good at acting.

He was taking a huge risk bringing Carlo to stay. There were, it was true, rumours round school that Marianne had a Thing going, or was *going* to have a Thing going with someone. He'd had to cover up for her a couple of times to put The Olds off the scent, so Laurie was doing what he always did – hoping for the best. Secretly, he feared that once his sister saw Carlo, the other guy would be history.

'You children,' Irene said, interrupting his thoughts, 'are up on the top floor. Laurence, show Carlo where the Brown Room is. You'll find a copy of the Work Rota pinned to the back of the door. I advise you to peruse it most carefully.

9

Then come down and we'll all have coffee and cake in the Chinese Lounge.'

'Right,' said Carlo. 'Thanks.'

Laurie supposed that he too wouldn't have had the heart to say no to Ellie when she bounded up and smiled at him and Carlo (but mainly at Carlo) and said: 'Can I come too? To show Carlo around, I mean. Please!'

The 'ee' of 'please' stretched out pathetically, and so of course Carlo said: 'Yes, come on. The more the merrier.'

'Follow me,' said Laurie, and they all went upstairs together.

'Didn't you promise me a Mad Conductor?' Carlo said. 'Where is he?'

'In his lonely garret,' said Laurie. 'Where else? But he'll come down when Nana brings out the cakes. No one can resist Nana's cooking.'

After that, Ellie took over and Laurie felt vaguely miffed. He'd been looking forward to this moment for weeks: taking Carlo through the Golden House, noticing what he said, how he reacted to everything and, above all, being alone with him. Now here was Ellie like some frisky Butlin's redcoat or something, telling Carlo more than he needed to know and not letting him, Laurie, get a word in edgeways. Carlo couldn't say much either, but he wandered through the corridors and up the staircases with his jaw dropping and his eyes swivelling all over the place to take in all the bits and pieces Ellie was pointing out.

'They made a film here once,' she said when she'd run out of architectural information. 'Ages ago. A horror film. I saw it once, when I was little, but you couldn't really

10

recognize the house. They'd put up sort of thingies on the wall that had torches stuck in them.'

'*Flickering* torches,' Laurie said. 'Horror movies are very big on flickering torches.'

'And ladies in nighties holding candles and going where you just *know* a vampire or something is waiting,' Carlo said.

'I've never understood that,' Laurie said, happy that the conversation was now moving away from Ellie's 'this is the Yellow Room' type of stuff. 'Any normal person would lock the door, pull the bedclothes over her head, and only wait till daybreak before getting the hell out of there, but, oh no, down the darkened corridors they go. They deserve to get their blood sucked. That's what I think.'

'You *have* to have dark corridors and monsters,' said Ellie. 'That's what the fun is. There wouldn't be a story if everybody just went home.'

'Would it matter?' Laurie said. 'If there were no story, I mean?'

'Of course it would matter,' said Ellie. 'I like stories. They always end happy ever after, even if horrible things happen first.'

'OK, OK,' Laurie laughed. 'I give up. Long live horror films and creepy tales.'

'Is there a real ghost?' Carlo wanted to know.

'It would be a brave ghost', said Laurie, 'that dared to tangle with Irene.'

'Tomorrow,' said Ellie, 'when it's light, I'll take you down to The Lake. That's haunted.'

'Tell me,' said Carlo.

'No,' said Ellie. 'You'll have to wait till tomorrow.' She

grinned and waved her fingers in front of her face and made the sort of noise little kids think of as spooky: 'Whoo . . . hoo . . . hoo!'

'Laurence, Carlo, Ellie!' Irene's voice carried up to them from downstairs. 'Coffee's ready. Come down, please.'

'Come on,' said Ellie, and she took Carlo's hand and practically pulled him along. Laurie followed them downstairs, filled with a sort of despairing envy. I should have done that, he thought. I wish I'd done that . . . taken Carlo's hand and held it. The thought of being able to do such a thing made him feel weak. He hesitated, leaning against the banister. When Ellie and Carlo reached the foot of the stairs, Carlo turned to look up at him.

'Laurie?' he said. 'What are you waiting for? Aren't you coming down?' He stretched out his hand and Laurie felt something . . . his heart? Could it possibly be? Doing a kind of somersault behind his ribcage.

'Try and stop me!' he said lightly, and thought: It's OK. It's going to be brilliant.

10.00 p.m. The Chinese Lounge

Carlo couldn't get over it. The Chinese Lounge was a room from one of Bette's magazines. For a start, it was huge. Our lounge at home, he thought, could probably fit into this space about four times. The ceilings were very high up and there were eight enormous windows all along one side of the room, with curtains Carlo had only ever seen in the theatre before: blood-coloured velvet, trimmed with gold braid near the hem.

At first, the only Chinese things he could see were the vases patterned with dark-blue dragons on either side of the fireplace. (Or urns? What on earth did you call them when they were as tall as a person?) Then he noticed the oriental designs on the rug in front of the fire and the pictures of long-legged birds and waterfalls on the pale-green walls.

'The tree's outside,' Irene said. 'In the big garage. Will you help me to bring it in, Derek, dear?'

'Leave it to me,' said Derek. 'I'll get it in before I go to bed.'

'Thank you,' said Irene. She was sitting on a sofa upholstered in some kind of shiny fabric the colour of a twopenny piece, and the Maestro was sitting next to her. He was harmless, of course, but a bit tapped for sure. Carlo obviously reminded him of someone he once knew, because he called him 'Alexei' and kept asking him where he'd put his violin.

Everyone chatted to him. Letta, Marianne and Laurie's mother asked him where he lived and did he have brothers and sisters, and Nana questioned him carefully about his favourite foods. Even Irene enquired about his mother and made him phone home. He'd been a little reluctant to do this . . . after all, he'd only just said goodbye . . . but Bette was, as she put it, 'thrilled skinny' to hear that he'd arrived safely. She'd seen a weather forecast and it was dreadful.

'I'll say Merry Christmas, Mum,' Carlo said.

'D'you know when you'll be back?'

'Not really,' he answered. 'I'll let you know after Christmas.'

What on earth had made him say that? He knew very well that the Springers were driving back on Boxing Day.

When he returned to the Chinese Lounge, they had all

made him feel at home, as if he were a member of their family. There was something to be said for not having a television. Everyone was talking to everybody else. Carlo thought of evenings when all that passed between him and his mother were remarks like: 'Pass the crisps' or 'What's on the other channels?' He wondered what he could say to Derek, who looked as though he might be coming over to him to start a conversation about the Repeal of the Corn Laws, or something. Carlo sighed and prepared to scintillate, but, fortunately, Carrie stopped Derek in his progress across the room, and so he was safe.

Laurie came and sat down on the floor beside his chair, and Carlo felt vaguely irritated because he had at that very moment been planning an expedition across miles and miles of floor and past crowds of people in an effort to sit next to Marianne. He suppressed his annoyance and began to talk to Laurie. After all, he said to himself, it's thanks to Laurie that I'm here at all. I'll talk to Marianne tomorrow. Carlo contented himself with gazing across the room at her, over Laurie's head, to see if he could make her look up, but all he got was Ellie, waving cheerily at him. She was nice enough, but still just a kid. He waved cheerily back, then turned his attention to Nana's delicious cinnamon-and-walnut pastry.

11.00 p.m. The Basement Flat
Nana had made up her mind not to say a word until after Christmas, and to hope that nothing unexpected happened that could draw attention to her and to how she felt. The day after Boxing Day, she would keep her appointment with the specialist. She'd already invented a meeting with

Greta, the only one of her old friends who was still alive. Till then, she would hang on. By hook or crook. Come what may.

Whenever she needed to take her mind off something unpleasant, she turned to food. Some people said prayers before they fell asleep, but nothing comforted Nana more than going through a mental list of what she had already prepared and stored in the three giant freezers and on the shelves of a pantry which was, in Marianne's words, 'as big as most people's bedrooms'. Sweet things were the most consoling. There were more than a hundred mince pies; cinnamon twists; apple strudels; and her own special Christmas flan, always eaten after the Midnight Service on Christmas Eve. It was baked in a huge silver tin that reminded her of the moon, and was a mixture of candied peel, pecan nuts and mincemeat left over from the pies, all cooked into a chewy toffee texture.

There were three enormous Christmas puddings, which she'd made in September and, of course, there was The Cake. That had been ready since October. The children were never in the house then, of course, and every year she had to bully Irene, Carrie and the Maestro into stirring the mixture and making a wish. She was the only one who still believed that cake-wishes could come true. The others just humoured her, she knew, but she didn't care.

She closed her eyes. The pain was on its way. Nothing must spoil the holiday for the babies. Laurie and Marianne and Ellie were almost grown up, but they would always be the babies to her. They must have a Christmas filled with all the good things that she could give them.

*

15

The winds swirl snow around the Golden House. The lawns, the lake and the dark trees look like a child's snow scene trapped in a bubble of glass where everything is iced with white.

Midnight. The Library

Ellie knelt up on the cushions of the window-seat and looked out at the garden and worried. She should have been asleep. She should have put her dressing gown and slippers on before wandering round the house in the dark.

'You heard me, didn't you, Pamina?' she whispered to the cat. 'They all think you do nothing but sleep, but it's not true. You know exactly what's going on. I know you do.'

Pamina jumped up beside her quite daintily, considering her weight and her great age. She settled herself next to Ellie, who began to stroke the pale-grey fur along her back. Soon the shadowy silence was filled with a liquid, melodious purring. The sound comforted Ellie. Maybe, she thought, there's nothing to worry about at all, but I can't help it. Sometimes she wondered if making a list of all the things that bothered her might help, but she was scared that writing down her troubles would make them even more . . . well, troublesome.

Top of the list, always top of the list, came her mother. She couldn't remember a time when she hadn't fretted about her. Was she OK? Would they be all right? When Dad left, everything got worse. She'd tried to be grown up about it and sophisticated, but secretly she hoped and prayed that her parents might get back together again. Once, she'd made the mistake of confiding this to Marianne, and her cousin

16

had advised her to 'get real'. It was easy for *her* to talk. There wasn't anything wrong with *her* life. She had both parents living with her, and everyone at school wanted to be her best friend. All Marianne had to do was be beautiful and ever-so-slightly aloof and dismissive of everyone, and they just carried on admiring her and hanging around waiting for the gift of her attention.

'And you're the worst, Elvira Bailey, so you can't complain.' She sighed. One of the things she liked best about Christmas was that it was a chance to be with Marianne. In her heart of hearts, Ellie knew her cousin was only ever chummy with her at the Golden House when there wasn't anyone more interesting around. At school, she thought, Marianne hardly ever comes near me, but here she never minds that I'm two years younger than she is.

For a moment Ellie thought about Carlo. What did Marianne think of him?

'I think he's really nice. And he's so gorgeous-looking, Pamina. I saw him staring at Marianne tonight. I bet he falls in love with her. I wish it was tomorrow. Maybe Mum has told Letta what the matter is and, if she has, then Marianne might know. Letta can't keep secrets. She talks too much.'

The cat looked at her in a bored sort of way, and licked her right front paw. Ellie stood up.

'OK,' she said. 'I can take a hint. I'm going to bed now.'

Pamina lifted her head briefly and watched Ellie leave the dark room. Then she turned her attention to the huge white moth-shapes blundering against the window pane. The snow was still falling. It was time to sleep.

Menus for the Day

LUNCH
Minestrone soup
Salads/cheeses/selected fresh bread
fresh and dried fruit

DINNER
Stuffed mushrooms
Aubergine tian with Lyonnaise potatoes
Broccoli
Apple-and-blackcurrant crumble

*

Coffee and petits fours

1.00 a.m. Irene's Room

Irene lay on the chaise longue in her room and thought about houses. She had given a name to every other bedroom, but her own was simply known as 'Irene's Room'. It was more than four walls and a door to her. She sometimes thought of it as a lair, and of herself as a wild creature who found in it both comfort and refuge. As for furnishings, she refused to limit herself to just one colour.

She had come to the conclusion that houses changed when everyone was in bed. When everything was quiet, the stones and the woodwork and the plaster and the beams moved and stretched and creaked. Draughts crept round half-closed doors and made the curtains shiver against the windows. Staircases turned up and up into shadow, and carpeted corridors slid between walls. Night lights made patches of blackness in unexpected corners. Houses settled down in the dark hours and waited for the dawn, which came late in winter.

Irene heard the branches of the laburnum tap against the glass of the Conservatory. She stood up and looked out of her window and sighed. Not a single star was visible, and the garden was lost in a cloud of snow. She went to her desk and took a document out of one of its hidden drawers. Here is something that no one knows about, she thought. Briefly, she wondered what secrets others in her family might be guarding. A house was always a kind of container: a big box in which to store everything – emotions, troubles, fears, dreams, desires, hopes, ambitions and, most of all, secrets.

She picked up her pen and signed her name. It will all change now, she said to herself. For all of us. Nothing in this family will ever be the same again. Never mind. Certain things needed to be changed.

Whenever she thought of the poor old Maestro and what she would have to tell him, her courage nearly failed her. But, she comforted herself, it will be for the best in the end. Soon Nana and I will be too old and feeble to look after him, and Carrie will be the one left to cope. There would be a certain justice to that, but Irene didn't believe in the young sacrificing themselves for the old. She wasn't sure, in fact, whether sacrifice in general was such a good thing.

She read the document once more, folded it and replaced

it in her desk. Then she took off her brocade robe (she had never in her life even *thought* 'dressing gown', much less *worn* a garment called by that name) and sat down on the bed. I shan't tell any of them anything yet, she thought. I shall wait until after Christmas.

2.00 a.m. The Brown Room

Carlo was breathing evenly, but Laurie couldn't sleep, which was a bit odd when you came to think about it. Carlo was the one in an unfamiliar bed, in a strange house. I'm too excited, Laurie thought. That's all. He tried to calm down by thinking of something mundane, like his presents. This year he'd made quantities of chocolate-covered orange peel. He'd sneaked out to put a big polythene bag full of it in the garage to keep cold. He would pack it in individual pretty boxes later . . . thank heavens they'd invented the kind that you assembled yourself, and that you could pack flat in your suitcase.

Every year, he loved the process of deciding what to make, unlike Marianne, who hated the whole business. She was so different from him in every way, that his mind turned to the endlessly fascinating subject of genes. How come, for instance, that his parents (dark, plump, chatty Letta and stringy, sandy, rather weedy Derek) could produce both tall, beautiful, red-headed Marianne and skinny, smallish, bespectacled and altogether ordinary Laurie? And what about Carlo? How could Bette ever have given birth to someone who only needed wings to be a dead ringer for the Archangel Gabriel? He pondered the puzzle of his aunts. Susanna had brown hair and brown eyes and brownish skin, and Carrie was painfully thin with gooseberry eyes and beige hair. Could you have beige hair? It was hard to know what else to call it. She wore it in a bun at the back of her neck, which made her look old-fashioned.

'She's nothing but a middle-aged hippie,' his mother always said. 'And why she thinks those long, trailing skirts do anything for her, I'll never know.'

He'd seen pictures of Irene when she was young, and it wasn't surprising that she was what was known in those days as 'a beauty'. No one said that nowadays. A babe, they'd say. Drop-dead gorgeous. Grandpa Ivor must have diluted the genes a bit, because although his mother and aunts were OK, none of them would exactly stop the traffic. Marianne would. Carlo thought so too, even though he hadn't said anything.

Laurie turned to look at him and wondered whether what he felt suddenly in the pit of his stomach was a pang of jealousy or too many slices of Nana's apple cake. Go to sleep, Laurie, he said to himself. He closed his eyes and turned to face the wall.

3.00 a.m. The White Room

Carrie had gone to bed early and fallen asleep, but the Maestro was up to his tricks again and that woke her up. By the time she'd got out of bed, gone downstairs to the Music Room and persuaded him that no, it wasn't time for his Chopin recital, and taken him back to his room, she was wide awake. Thank goodness she'd found him while he was pottering around and before he'd started to play.

The others are dutiful, Carrie thought, but I'm the only one who really loves him. True, it was the kind of love you felt for a shaggy old dog who's been with you for years, but it was love nonetheless. I'm an expert on love, Carrie said to herself, and laughed out loud. How amazed her mother and sisters would be if she said such a thing to them.

Once she was back in her room, she tried to sleep and failed. Never mind, she thought. I can do something useful. She made herself a pot of peppermint tea and sat down at her desk. Beside her on a table were two piles of identical small books and she was going to write a personal message on the title page of each one. She stroked the dust jacket as she opened the first book, and smiled when she thought of what they'd all say. At first, no one would believe it. Her sisters would cry: 'Why didn't you tell us, Carrie?' She'd just smile enigmatically. She always smiled enigmatically. She did it both when she didn't know what to say and when she knew what to say, but didn't feel like saying it.

Not many people understood her. They thought her peculiar. Mysterious.

'Why hasn't she married like a normal person?' was the question that hovered over the head of everyone she met, but was never uttered. Carrie could almost see it. She imagined it enclosed in a sort of pinkish balloon. She laughed out loud. If only they knew! Well, Carrie thought, I'd rather appear mysterious than foolish. She blew on the black words her pen had written, to help the ink dry. Tomorrow she would wrap each book in mauve tissue paper and tie the parcels up with silver string.

This is what some people say when it snows: there's an old woman plucking geese in the sky. Maybe it's true, because here they are: feathers and more freezing feathers blown against the glass and blurring every sharp edge that they touch.

7.00 a.m. The Pink Room

Marianne had managed to prop open the door of her cupboard in a way that allowed her to see at least a slice of herself as she went through her barre exercises. It wasn't a proper barre, of course, but the brass rail at the foot of her bed. Thank heavens, she thought, for small mercies. There were some good things about being stuck in a five-star mausoleum. En-suite bathroom and coffee-making stuff in your room . . . those were great, but why wasn't there colour TV as well? I'd insist on one, she thought, especially at Irene's prices.

She knew her exercise routine by heart. She didn't want the others waking up, so the music from the tape in her ghetto blaster was turned down as low as it would go before disappearing.

'Ghetto whisperer,' Marianne intoned quietly, and continued, to the rhythm of her movements, with a list of synonyms for 'Boring'.

'Te-dious. Mind-crush. Numb-ing. Snore-ish. Yawn-y. No films. No clubs. No shops. No fun.'

The music changed tempo then and Marianne bent from the waist over and over again, sweeping her fingers along the carpet and almost kissing her knees. She smiled. I could, she thought, liven things up . . . all I have to do is tell Mum and Dad and everyone else exactly what I'm going to do after the exams next summer, perhaps just as we're sitting down to one of Nana's endless feasts, and there would be a real chandelier-rattler of a row.

Most people, Marianne knew, shrank from such a prospect. Ellie would turn herself inside out to avoid a quarrel, and Laurie went all pale and sickly at the first whiff of trouble. But I'm not scared of fights, she thought. Maybe I quite enjoy them. Perhaps this Christmas wouldn't be exactly the same as all the others, but some things, she was sure, would never change: endless food she didn't want to eat, the stupid Work Rota, which was like the Ten Commandments or something, and the Home-made Presents nonsense, which became more and more irksome every year. This time she had embroidered strips of canvas with tiny tapestry stitches to be bookmarks . . . it would have been so much simpler to go and buy gift tokens for everybody, but the traditions had to be upheld.

Then there was Ellie running round after her. Ellie was all right, but such devotion was tiring. The grown-ups would be doing their thing: five minutes under their mother's roof and they became kids again, back to jostling for Irene's attention. Susanna looked ill, and what did Carrie suddenly have to be so pleased about? What on earth did she do all day? Did she *really* enjoy mooching round this gloomy pile like some heroine from a horror movie? Had anyone else noticed that she rarely left the house and hadn't been further than the village in ten years? Didn't that count as a kind of agoraphobia? Why was nothing done about it? Or maybe Irene had tried and failed? Carrie was famously pig-headed. Marianne's thoughts turned to Carlo . . . he might turn out to be fun, even though that blond, wishy-washy style wasn't really her sort of thing. I wonder, she thought, if he knows how much Laurie likes him? I wonder if even Laurie knows that.

The tape ended and she looked at her bedside clock. Not even half-past seven: practically the middle of the night. She went to the window and pulled aside the pink-velvet curtain, thinking: I wouldn't mind a dress made out of this. Frost had arranged itself in a lace pattern round the edges of every pane, but she could see enough.

'Bloody snow!' she muttered. Talk about a Worst Case Scenario! Everyone else went quite soppy about it, and words like 'pure' and 'white' and 'magical' and 'hushed' were used.

'Slushed, more like,' Marianne said. And, she thought, cold and wet and give-you-pneumonia-soon-as-look-at-you. And hold-up-the-trains-and-stop-people-going-where-they-want-to-go. A chill settled on Marianne's heart. Was it possible they wouldn't be able to go home on Boxing Day? This was way beyond Worst Case Scenario, and she thrust it firmly from her mind. She wouldn't even *half-think* such dreadful things just in case, by allowing them room in her head, she somehow made them happen.

Instead, she thought of Andy. He was dark and stocky, with eyes that her best friend, Stacey, called 'burning'. Definitely her type. No one knew about him, not even Laurie. She was pretty sure of that. He was her secret so far and, even though she'd needed Laurie to cover for her with Mum and Dad a couple of times, he didn't know exactly what was going on. Marianne smiled. Nothing *was* going on anywhere really except in her head, but that was all set to change. He had asked her to the Boxing Day disco at La Bodega.

'You'll be there, yeah?' he'd said, and just remembering what his eyes looked like when he said it made her feel hot and cold and faint. She *would* be there. It'd be fine. They'd leave here after tea on Boxing Day and be home by seven or so. Nothing serious happened at La Bodega till after ten. If The Olds knew, they would get all parental and heavy. Marianne could almost hear them . . . the young man who works *where?* At the newsagent's? An all-night disco? At your age? Horrors and double horrors!

She smiled. She'd thought of all that. She was spending the night at Stacey's house. That was the story. It was all fixed up. Now it was just a matter of getting through Christmas. She'd be extra sweet and helpful. No making of waves. A good girl, she thought. I can be one of those for three days.

She glanced out of the window. The gazebo looked like an ice-palace, the white wrought iron even whiter than usual, and the long windows frosted and opaque. Then she saw . . . she rubbed the pane to make sure she was seeing properly. Someone, a woman, was making her way towards the house through the snow, looking like something out of a Victorian melodrama. Who was it, coming to visit them before it was even light? No, it wasn't . . . it couldn't be. It was. The woman was her own mother, doing a very passable imitation of Good King Wenceslas.

Whatever was she up to? Letta was someone who never willingly stepped into the open air. In another age, she'd have been one of those ladies who sat up in vast beds all morning, wearing frilly things and eating breakfast from a silver tray, while fluffy animals of one kind or another lounged around on the elegantly rumpled satin counterpane. Now she was at the back door. She's looking around quite guiltily, Marianne thought. Why? I'll see if she says anything at breakfast. What if she doesn't? What would that mean? Marianne turned away from the window and peeled off her leotard as she walked to the shower. Curiouser and curiouser, she thought, and then: I wish it would stop snowing.

8.00 a.m. The Dining Room

There were far too many humans in the house. They seemed to be on every chair and walking about between the sideboard and the table. Pamina liked to start her day here on the wide window sill because, if the sun was out, pale-yellow light flooded this room. There was no sunlight today, as far as she could see, and the garden had vanished. Outside had turned into whiteness and more whiteness. Pamina decided to move to the Conservatory, which was always warm and often deserted. She made her way carefully to the door, with her plume-like tail whisking the carpet behind her. Every day, it became harder and harder to stay awake.

9.00 a.m. The Dining Room

'Napoleon', said Derek through a mouthful of Weetabix, 'and Hitler...' (pausing for two or three thoughtful chewings) '... were both vanquished by the snow.'

'Oh, God, Dad!' said Laurie. 'Please, not Napoleon. And please, please not Hitler! Not at breakfast.' He turned to his boiled egg.

Carlo had taken the chair next to Marianne. He thought: breakfasts like this only happen in soap operas, surely? Even the dialogue was a little unreal. Who on earth, apart from Derek, would have said 'vanquished' instead of 'beaten'? Marianne smiled at her mother.

'By the way, Mum,' she said, 'talking of snow, what on

27

earth were you doing tramping across it at crack of dawn? I saw you coming back from the village.'

Carlo was sure that someone had once told Letta she had a silvery laugh. Or possibly a bell-like one, because she made a meal of it, trilling away for far too long.

'What nonsense, Marianne,' she said finally. 'As if I'd go out at that hour, even in summer. It must have been someone else. Or you were half asleep and still dreaming.'

Marianne stared at her mother, who was rather pink in the face. Then she turned to Carlo and whispered under her breath: 'She's lying, of course. That's obvious to anyone. Why does she feel she needs to, though? The plot thickens . . .'

She quartered an apple very precisely and arranged the pieces artistically on her plate with a few satsuma segments and some pale discs of banana.

'There's no need for you to make that face,' she said to her mother. 'I'm not going to change my habits just because it's Christmas. I always have fruit only for breakfast.'

Letta opened her mouth and was about to say something when the doorbell rang.

'It's the postman!' Ellie cried. 'I'll go and see what he's got.'

She ran out of the room. Marianne glanced at Carlo and said: 'Ellie's waiting for a parcel from her dad, only he's such a no-hoper he'll have put the wrong postage on it or something and her present will probably roll up in February.'

'Why isn't he here?' Carlo asked.

'Divorced,' Marianne said, 'and gone to America with his new wife.'

Carlo would have asked for more details, but Ellie was at the door. She said: 'Look, everyone! Look who's come for breakfast! It's Edmund.'

The man standing behind her looked to Carlo as though he'd been sleeping in his clothes for days.

'Who's that?' he whispered to Marianne. 'And what's he doing with that baby?'

'Sssh!' said Marianne. 'That's Edmund. He's the vet. He lives down in the village in a hideous old house called The Gables, that's also his surgery. Something must have happened. That's his baby. She's only about six weeks old. Men *are* allowed to hold babies . . . didn't you know?'

'Edmund, dear,' said Irene, rising from the table and going to him. 'Where's Serena? Is anything wrong? Come and sit down . . . sit here.'

'Serena's gone,' said Edmund, allowing himself to be led to a chair.

'Nana, dear, take the baby,' said Irene.

Nana moved at once, making sorrowful crooning noises: 'Come, baby darling . . . come to your Nana.'

As soon as the child was taken from his arms, Edmund put his hands over his face and began to weep.

'I can't,' he said. 'I cannot bear it . . . no.'

'Ellie, my love,' said Irene, 'you go and help Nana settle the baby down. You're so good with little children . . . go on, now. She'll need your help.'

'Transparent,' Marianne whispered to Carlo. 'She wants Ellie out of the room before Edmund says anything. And Ellie wants to go and help with the kid because she's soppy about things like that, but she's nosy too. Look, she's signalling to me . . . can you see?'

29

Marianne nodded and mouthed the words: 'I'll tell you later' at Ellie as she and Nana left the room.

'Now, my dear,' said Irene. 'Your baby is in good hands. Have a warm drink and tell us everything.'

Carrie had already poured a cup of coffee and was standing in front of Edmund and leaning over him a little.

'You're very kind, Carrie,' he said, looking up at her. And Marianne was astonished to see her aunt blushing and staring down at the carpet. How peculiar, she thought. Carrie was obviously what her mother called a dark horse.

9.15 a.m. The Landing and the Basement Flat
Ellie followed Nana upstairs and sighed. They'd shut the dining-room door and now there wasn't even a tiny chance of voices reaching her.

'Here we are,' said Nana, a little out of breath. 'Just help me get a nice blanket out.'

Ellie opened the enormous dark cupboard that stood at the end of the first-floor corridor. All the blankets (apricot, pale green and cream) were neatly lined up with the edges of the shelves. Nana made a 'tsk-ing' noise.

'Look at those. Enough for fifteen beds, only we have duvets these days, of course. Still, you know your grandmother. She keeps everything. Now, let's take this child to my room and see what needs to be done.'

'Where do you think Edmund's wife has gone?' Ellie asked as they went down to Nana's bedroom in the basement. 'How could she leave little Olivia?'

Nana sniffed. 'I've never liked that name. It's too grown up for a baby. Just put her here on the bed, dear.'

'She won't always be a baby, Nana.'

Olivia began to cry quietly, and beat the air with her tiny hands.

'Are you sure she won't roll off?' Ellie asked, looking at the baby lying on the puffy quilt.

'She's much too young to roll about, God bless her,' said Nana.

'I had a doll when I was small who was about that size . . . she's so tiny. I've never seen such a little baby.'

Ellie closed her eyes quickly to stop herself from crying. Until her dad left, she used to wish for a baby sister every single night of her life, and one of the worst things about losing him was knowing that she would now always, always be an only child. She opened her eyes and leaned over to whisper in the baby's ear.

'I wish you were mine, little baby. I wish you could live with me forever.'

'There's plenty we don't know about,' said Nana, breaking into Ellie's thoughts, 'and more that isn't our business, but this child needs changing.'

'Edmund brought a rucksack. It's by the front door. I bet there are nappies in it.'

'I don't hold with those newfangled nappies,' said Nana. 'I'm sure we've still got some proper towelling ones somewhere . . .'

'Sssh, Olivia,' Ellie said. 'I'll go and see what's in your daddy's bag. We'll look after you. You'll be fine.'

Work Rota: Letta and Derek

Letta was washing the dishes and Derek was drying them. This was the way they organized things in their own house because, according to Letta, all Derek was capable of was vaguely waggling plates and cups about in soapy water and hoping for the best.

'I'm, on the other hand,' she often said, 'someone who goes right down between the tines of a fork.'

'Few people,' Derek was in the habit of answering, 'even know the word "tine", and it is a rare and courageous soul who actually ventures between them to seek out encrustations of egg yolk and other nightmares.'

Derek was a slow and thoughtful drier-up.

'Get a move on,' Letta said, 'or we'll be here all day.'

Derek took no notice, but went on gently stroking cereal bowls and arranging them on the table in neat piles. He said mildly: 'It's not as though we've got a thousand things to do when this is over, is it? Thank God for the Work Rota, that's what I say. And do you know that even though it *looks* unfair . . . you're on lunch duty today, for instance . . . Irene always sees to it that we do the same number of shifts.'

'Carrie does the Rota,' Letta muttered. 'Not Irene. It's a fairly simple matter to get it to come out fair, I'd have thought. Anyway . . .' She swished her hands (encased in rubber gloves – she wasn't going to risk chapped skin and broken nails) in the soapy water and frowned – 'you're only wittering on about the Work Rota because you don't want to talk about it.'

'Quite right,' said Derek. 'I don't. I shall try not to think about it either until we get home, though that of course will be much harder. In fact . . .' He hung another teacup from a hook on the dresser. 'I find it difficult to think about anything else.'

'Oh, Derek, Stop!' Letta pulled the plug and waited for

the water to twist down the drain. 'I feel so awful, but it's . . . well, it's an overwhelming thing, can't you see? I never asked for it, but it happened and that's all there is to it, and the very last thing I want is to hurt you and the children.'

Derek laughed. 'Oh, Letta darling, anything but the platitudes, please. At least spare me those. Be honest. You *have* hurt me. You *will* hurt the children. Your new love is evidently so great that you reckon our pain is a price you are willing to pay. So be it, but don't pretend you care about me. Not at this stage.'

Letta's knuckles were white with anger as she wiped the stainless steel surfaces round the sink.

'I refuse,' she said, 'to get into another fight. There are too many people in this house, and heaven knows we don't want to rock the Christmas boat, do we?'

'I think it may already be too late,' Derek said, beginning to put all the dishes away in the cupboards. 'Marianne saw you coming back from the village this morning. I don't for a moment think she believed you at breakfast when you denied it. You should have seen yourself – guilt personified. I suppose you were phoning him, though why you couldn't have done so from the house, I can't imagine.'

'I know,' said Letta. 'That's exactly what's wrong with you. You really *can't* imagine anything, can you? Not anything. Not one thing. You are totally lacking in imagination. I went to the village because anyone at all in this house could have picked up an extension at any time and listened in.'

'I hope the conversation was worth getting up before dawn and tramping across the snow for,' said Derek.

'It wasn't, as it happens. The phone box was out of order.'

'Oh, dear,' said Derek. 'How frightful for you!'

'Don't,' said Letta. 'I beg you. Don't try being sarcastic. It doesn't suit you.'

'What doesn't suit him?' said Laurie, who had wandered into the kitchen at that moment.

'Nothing,' said Letta, brushing past him on her way out. 'It's none of your concern.'

'Who rattled her cage?' Laurie stared at his mother's back as she hurried up the stairs at the end of the corridor. 'I was only bringing in my cup to be washed.'

'Rattled her cage,' said Derek. 'A disgusting expression, but very vivid. I think I'm probably the one.'

He looked so glum that Laurie laughed.

'Cheer up, Dad,' he said. 'It's nearly Christmas.'

Derek stopped himself from saying something like: I'll be heartily glad when the whole thing's over, and said instead: 'Ah, yes, Christmas! Let joy be unconfined and so on. I can hardly wait.'

As he watched Laurie washing his own cup in the sink, he wondered why it was that he so seldom said what was in his mind. The next few days would be more than the usual gift-wrapped, tinsel-strewn tedium of what people *would* call The Festive Season. His misery would sit like a stone at the heart of everything. Still, Letta is right, he thought, about one thing. The children mustn't know till we get home. Let them be carefree while they can.

11.00 a.m. The Basement Flat

'What on earth are you doing in Nana's room?' Marianne said. 'I've been looking for you all over the house. Irene

34

wants us to go up to the attic and get the stuff so that I can make a start on the tree.'

'I've been helping Nana with Olivia . . . the baby.'

'That was *hours* ago. They've been chewing over poor Edmund for ages. I got bored in the end.' Marianne looked briefly over to the bed. 'The baby's asleep. There's nothing for you to do, is there?'

'No,' said Ellie. She decided to change the subject. 'What happened? To Mrs Edmund, I mean.'

'She'd had enough, apparently,' said Marianne, 'and I can't say that I blame her. Stuck out in the middle of the wilderness and not even a supermarket to cheer her up. *And* her front room being a surgery for sick cats and dogs, *and* a husband out in the fields with cows and things, *and* a bawling infant wrecking her love life. I'd be off like a shot myself.'

Ellie sighed. She knew that it would have been impossible to explain to her cousin why it was that she found it so easy to sit and stare at Olivia. Perhaps she wouldn't even have been able to explain it to herself. She stood up and said: 'We'd better go then. Irene'll be after us if we hang about. But when will you tell me what Edmund said? I do want to know.'

They left Nana's bedroom and made their way upstairs.

'It wasn't very interesting.' Marianne shrugged. 'Honestly. I think he was saying as little as he possibly could. He sniffed a lot and did loads of sighing, but from what I can gather, Serena just didn't fancy him any more.'

'Did she fall in love with someone else?'

'He never said.'

'She must have done,' said Ellie. 'She must have loved

35

this other person heaps, otherwise she couldn't have left Olivia.'

'Has it ever occurred to you,' said Marianne as she opened the door of the Chinese Lounge, ready to look at the tree, 'that Serena might have been glad to see the back of that baby?'

'Never!' Ellie was shocked. 'She couldn't have been. She's Olivia's mother.'

'Grow up, Ellie!' Marianne was scornful. 'Didn't you know? There *is* such a thing as mothers who aren't totally besotted with their kids. Now.' She gazed at the tree, which stood like some wild, green creature in the corner, uneasy among the brocade slip covers and tall blue-and-white pottery vases. 'What's it to be this year? What can I do to dazzle the assembled multitudes?'

Ellie turned away. I shan't let her get to me, she thought. Part of her knew that Marianne was right about mothers, but surely, surely most people weren't like that? I won't be, she vowed silently. When I have a baby, I'll love it better than anything else in the whole world.

'I don't know,' she said. 'You decide. It's always lovely whatever you do.'

The tree tradition was one of the things Ellie liked best about Christmas. Marianne had been in charge of the decorations ever since she was eight. That year, she had torn all the tinsel and baubles off the branches in the middle of the night because, in her words, 'they looked so ugly'.

Irene, instead of punishing her, had said: 'You're quite right. It looks ghastly. You can be responsible for making it beautiful from now on.'

So now, Marianne did something different and amazing

36

every year. She worked in the Chinese Lounge with the curtains pulled across the windows. No one else was allowed to see anything until Christmas morning. Wrapped presents were left in the Front Hall on Christmas Eve and, just before she went to bed, Marianne arranged them under the lowest branches.

'I'm running out of ideas,' Marianne said. 'In any case, I'll have to go up to the attic. Coming?'

'No,' said Ellie, still feeling aggrieved, though she wouldn't have been able to say why exactly, if anyone had asked her. There had been something she didn't like in Marianne's voice a moment ago. Almost, Ellie said to herself, as though she were scornful of me being so anxious about the baby and so interested in her. Well, she can get knotted. I'm not going to help her with the stupid tree. I don't care whether it gets decorated or not.

'I'll help you,' said Carlo. He'd been sitting on the sofa, but Marianne hadn't given any sign of having seen him, and she'd certainly not spoken to him.

Now she smiled and said: 'Thanks, Carlo. There's always tons of stuff to bring down, and attics are fun, aren't they? Full of secrets. Follow me.'

Carlo stood up at once, looking, Ellie thought, as though he would gladly follow Marianne to the ends of the earth. Now that he was going as well, she was longing to say that yes she would come after all, but it was too late. They'd already left, and the Chinese Lounge was empty except for Pamina, curled up against the turquoise satin sofa cushions.

'Rats, Pamina! That's what I say. Rats and double rats! She can stew in her own juice. I'm going to see how deep the snow is.'

11.30 a.m. The Attic

'It's exactly . . .' Carlo began, and then fell silent.

'Exactly what?' Marianne had crossed the floor of the attic and opened a tall chest of drawers that stood against one of the walls.

'Nothing,' said Carlo. 'It doesn't matter.'

He stared at everything, not quite believing his eyes. An attic. He'd often imagined it. It was part of being a Real Family in a Real House. They always had attics in books and movies where they needed to show that the people in the story had a history. This attic was perfect. It had to be the most attic-y attic in the world. Everything that should have been up there actually was: an old rocking horse with the gold flake chipped off the red saddle; a cliff face of piled-up suitcases and boxes; an enormous trunk like something from a theatrical production of *Treasure Island*, with a domed lid bound with wooden hoops; and, in one corner, a gathering of old chairs and sofas, ghostly in pale dust sheets.

'That's it,' said Marianne. 'That's the box I need. The striped one . . . the hatbox. We're going to have to lift these others.'

'I'll do it,' said Carlo. I'd do anything, he thought, as he picked up one suitcase after another and put it down on the floor. I'd break rocks. I'd swim rivers. Anything.

'Great!' said Marianne. 'Thanks. That's the one. My dear grandmother's done her best to hide it away, but I've found it. I knew it'd be up here.'

'What's in it?'

'Ribbons. I've just had an idea.'

Carlo frowned. 'Is this whole box full of ribbons?'

'Yes . . . there's thousands of them. Well, hundreds anyway.'

'But why? Why would anyone have so many?'

'Because Irene collected them for years and years. They were once tied around bouquets of flowers and boxes of chocolates and perfume, and unpicked from costumes and, oh, I don't know . . . all sorts of stuff. She showed them all to me once. She can remember with some of them the exact occasion and the person who gave her the flowers or whatever. Look.'

Marianne took off the lid of the hatbox.

'I never expected them to be . . .' Carlo hesitated.

'So tidy,' said Marianne. 'I know. I used to imagine the Ribbon Box like a sort of nest of satin and velvet snakes, all squirming around together. They look a bit like cotton reels, don't they? But . . .' She giggled and pulled out a scarlet streamer and shook it in Carlo's face. '. . . they become snaky.'

The ribbon trailed across his cheek and he caught a faint sweet fragrance. Did it come from the satin, or was it from Marianne? He said: 'No one gets as many bunches of flowers as this. Or boxes of chocolates, come to that.'

'Irene did. She was famous. A dozen bouquets on stage every night sometimes, so she says.'

'Famous? What for?' Carlo asked.

'Hasn't Laurie told you?'

'No.'

'Typical.' Marianne sighed. 'My brother never knows what to tell and what to leave out. Irene used to be an opera singer. She was really famous. Ask anyone. Irene Golden. It was a brilliant name for headlines. You can work

39

out for yourself the earth shatteringly original things the papers came up with: "The Golden Voice", et cetera. That big trunk's full of old costumes. I used to love them when I was little. In fact I . . .' She stopped.

'What?'

'Nothing. Never mind. Let's go down. They'll be wondering where we've got to.'

She had nearly, very nearly, told him something. Something private and important to her. Should he ask her about it? Pretend it never happened? Say something to change the subject?

'Here,' he said in the end, picking up the red ribbon from where it had fallen on the dusty floor. 'Don't forget this one.'

Carlo took a step closer to Marianne and put it round her neck like a scarf, with the two ends dangling down over her grey sweatshirt.

'Beautiful,' he whispered. Marianne looked at the floor, then she looked at him and grinned and stepped away.

'Just the thing to complete my fashionable outfit,' she said lightly, turning everything normal again. For a second or two there had been a weight and a density to the air that made Carlo feel breathless. He followed her downstairs, carrying the hatbox. Part of something that was *almost* said; part of something that had *nearly* happened was left up there with the other ghosts, and another fragment was in his head. Later he would unwind and rewind the time in the attic as though it were one of Irene's ribbons, and look at it all over again.

12.00 noon. The Chinese Lounge

Marianne put the hatbox down next to the tree and thought about Carlo. She took the ribbon he'd hung around her neck and ran it hard through her fingers so that it sprang into a curl. It wasn't as though she'd forgotten about Andy, but he was in town and Carlo was here. It was all Irene's fault for not allowing TV. If we were watching silly films, there'd be less time for mooching about. It needn't mean anything. It could be like a holiday romance . . . something to make time pass more pleasantly, which would come to a natural end when we go home.

12.00 noon. The Kitchen

Laurie was pretending to be listening to music. He had his earphones in, but there was no tape in his Walkman. Tee hee, he thought. There's nothing like a Nook (unless, of course, it's a Cranny) for the eager eavesdropper and this kitchen was full of them. The battered sofa that used to be in the Library had been moved down here, and Nana had put it in a corner. You could lie on it and, if you were silent enough, anyone sitting at the kitchen table would very soon forget that you were there. The headphones were added insurance. Susanna was on the pre-lunch Work Rota with Letta, and this included peeling potatoes, ready for dinner.

'I can't imagine,' said Letta, 'why everyone doesn't use frozen stuff. I really can't. And if potatoes *do* need peeling, then where are the children? Why can't they do it? It oughtn't to be part of the Work Rota, surely? Laurie?'

Nana said: 'He can't hear a thing. And, anyway, I don't want that young man anywhere near my potatoes. He doesn't peel them so much as take chunks out of them.'

After a few moments, Laurie thought: if the conversation doesn't improve, I'm off. If there are to be no spillings of beans or unburdenings of the heart, I'll go and do something else. He ignored an inner voice that was saying: What? What exactly will you do? Marianne is in the Chinese Lounge with the door closed doing private artistic things to the tree, and Carlo and Ellie seem to have disappeared. He considered going to look for Carlo, but then he tuned in again to what was going on at the table. Aha! They were discussing Carrie. This would be fun. There's an iron law for brothers and sisters when they number more than two: whenever Sibling A and Sibling B are gathered together, the talk will be of Sibling C.

'She always was,' said Letta, 'absolutely soppy over him. Don't you remember his wedding?'

'Vaguely,' said Susanna. 'Carrie vanished. She was supposed to be a bridesmaid, and she disappeared.'

'That's right.' Letta laughed. 'I had to stand in for her at the last minute and I felt completely ridiculous in her dress. I've never forgiven her.'

'Where was she?' Susanna said. 'I've forgotten.'

'How could you have? She was locked in the upstairs bathroom, weeping and wailing. She wouldn't come out. Mother spent half the afternoon whispering into the keyhole. Carrie only emerged after the reception was over and Edmund and Serena had left.'

So that was it, Laurie thought. Carrie used to be in love with Edmund. He'd broken her heart. But had he? Maybe she'd just withered away in silent longing and he knew nothing about her loving him. Totally fascinating. He willed them to say a little more. He listened.

'Well,' his mother said, 'she's got him here now.'

'What ever do you mean? Surely Mother hasn't—'

'She has,' Letta said. 'She's invited him to stay for Christmas. I heard her. "Dearest Edmund," she says, "I know that Mr Teasland is looking after the surgery over Christmas . . . I asked him about Pamina only the other day . . . but you have quite enough to worry about without thinking of domestic arrangements. Of course you must stay here. We will all love having you and it's many years since we had a baby in the house at Christmas. It'll be a pleasure for us." *I* wanted to say: but not one of us has a present for him, but Mother got in first, naturally. "We'll give you a cheque for the Animal Shelter as a present," she says and puts on that "I'm completely irresistible to men" look that she's used for forty years. Naturally Edmund gallantly says that just her hospitality is present enough, and so on till we're all bored to tears.'

Laurie just happened to be looking at his aunt as his mother was speaking. Letta was never aware of the effect she was having, but *he* saw. Susanna put down the potato peeler and wiped the tip of her finger across the corner of her eye. First one eye, then the other. She looked as though . . . she couldn't be, could she? Now she was blinking very quickly. She was, she definitely was, trying to stop herself crying. Why? Letta was still talking.

'So I said to her, "Mother, that makes us thirteen . . . it's very unlucky." And do you know what she had the cheek to say? You'll never guess. She just smiled at me and said, exactly as though I were about eight years old . . . she said, "Fourteen, Violetta. I hope you aren't thinking of excluding darling Pamina from the family?" Isn't that

43

typical of Mother? Susanna? Is something wrong? Susanna, is it something I said?'

Oh, so she's noticed, Laurie thought. Not surprising, really. Susanna had lost the battle with her tears. She sat at the table with both hands plunged in the basin of water and potato peelings and her cheeks were wet.

'I'm sorry . . . I'm so sorry,' she kept saying. 'I don't know why I'm crying . . . I don't really. No, Letta, it isn't you, truly. It's nothing. I don't . . . I can't . . . I'm going to wash my face before Ellie sees me. She mustn't know I was in this state . . . Letta, promise me. Will you promise? Not a word to Ellie . . . it's nothing, but you know how she worries.'

Susanna stood up and ran from the room, leaving Letta and Nana with open mouths.

'Has she said anything to you, Nana?' Letta asked.

'Not a word,' said Nana. 'Not a single word.' She shook her head. 'Perhaps she's sickening for something.'

Nana always says that, Laurie thought. And less than a heartbeat after thinking it, he heard his mother say: 'You *always* say that, Nana. You just say it for something to say. It's obvious that Susanna's unhappy, but you don't like to face things.'

She flounced out of the room after her sister. Now Nana was looking miserable. What if she starts bawling too? Laurie decided diversionary tactics were called for.

He took off his earphones and said: 'I see your helpers have deserted you, Nana. D'you want me to go on with the spuds?'

'No, thank you, Laurie darling,' Nana said. 'I'll be

quicker on my own. And it's nearly time for lunch. Off you go.'

Laurie went. That, he decided, was a good bit of spying. Who should he tell? And what should he tell them? And what about Ellie? Ought she to know about her mother? A knotty moral problem, Laurie thought. Spies were forever dealing with those.

12.45 p.m. The Lake

Ellie stood on the white slope overlooking the Lake and clapped her hands to try and keep warm. Carlo hadn't come to find out about the Lake. They called it that, even though it was more like a pond, because it was haunted and you couldn't have, Marianne said, a haunted pond. It didn't sound right.

Carrie had told her the story ages ago and Ellie had passed it on to her cousins. A housemaid, left in charge of twin girls, had turned her back for a moment and one child had drowned, even though the water was shallow. Carrie said that, on summer nights, you could sometimes hear sobbing. That was the housemaid or the twin who survived, no one really knew.

Ellie wasn't a bit scared, because they were summer ghosts. She stamped her feet. He's probably mooching around after Marianne. Typical. *Everyone* mooches around after her. I don't care. I just wish my wellingtons were fur-lined, she thought. I wish I had a pound for every time I said 'I wish' in my head. I must be the most dissatisfied person in the whole world, always wanting and wanting things.

'Things I can't have,' she said aloud, and her words hung

in the air, floating on the white vapour that curled out of her mouth like smoke. She turned towards the house. It was no good. No one had missed her. No one was coming to see where she was. For all they knew, she had twisted her ankle and was lying stiff and blue in a snowdrift somewhere, and a fat lot they cared. Marianne was doing the tree, and Laurie and Carlo had gone off to do something or other. Nana was busy cooking or changing Olivia's nappy, and all the grown-ups were too busy mooching about to wonder where she'd gone.

But my own mother, she thought (and just thinking the words made her feel like crying), my own mother should care. As miserable as she is, she ought to think: What's happened to Ellie? She must know how awful I feel. This was, after all, the first Christmas that she would be spending without her father. She thought of him, far away on the other side of the world, and just the *distance* there was between them made her want to cry. Susanna said that she could phone him on Christmas Day, and she'd spent ages thinking of everything she wanted to tell him, but she knew that it wouldn't be like that. Somehow, on the telephone, nothing was quite real. She didn't sound like herself and neither did he. All the words came out stiff, and you weren't allowed to shout and scream and say what you really wanted to say – Daddy, I miss you. Where are you? Come home. *How could you leave me?*

Quite suddenly she realized how hungry she was. No wonder. She'd run out of breakfast to open the door to Edmund, and never gone back. She tried to remember what the menu for lunch was. It wasn't a sit-down meal, but a buffet of delicious bits and bobs. Ellie looked at the Golden

House against the grey sky, and thought that if she were writing a story about it, she'd say it was 'looming'. Looming was a good word and it was something the Golden House did a lot, even in warm weather. In this freezing landscape, it looked like a rest home for retired vampires. Ellie giggled. She found her own witticisms hilarious, but wondered whether this one was funny enough to pass on . . . Laurie would like it, she decided, and Marianne would think it was silly.

As she approached, the Golden House loomed a little less. Now, she thought, it looks like a doll's house. She peered through the panel of opaque, bubbled yellow glass set into the front door. Letta was talking on the phone. You could hear her even through the door. She sounded upset. Who on earth could she possibly be talking to? Everyone in her family was already here. Perhaps Marianne might know. Ellie pushed open the door. Letta put the phone down immediately, right in the middle of what she was saying.

'Goodness,' she said. 'I've been cut off.'

But she hadn't. Ellie was quite sure that she'd slammed down the handset the minute she saw the front door opening.

In midwinter, the sun glows with a pearly orange radiance as it slides towards the horizon, and shadows on the snow are mauve or deep purple. Darkness comes quickly.

3.00 p.m. The Garden

'How much longer,' said Marianne, breathing on her gloved hands, 'is this torture going to continue?'

Ellie laughed. 'It's not torture, Marianne. It's fun.' She smiled at her cousin and turned back to her task: adding more snow to what had become the Snow Lady's bustle. 'Everyone always makes snowmen. That's what you're meant to do when it snows.'

'No,' said Marianne, stamping her feet, which had turned, she was convinced, into pure ice. 'When it snows, especially at Christmas, you're meant to sit in front of the telly and watch crappy movies and try and break the crisp-eating record and only move from the roaring fire to go to the fridge for more Coke.'

'But isn't she beautiful?' Carlo asked. 'Our Snow Lady?'

'She's OK,' Marianne said grudgingly. 'Ellie's good at making things. It's in her genes. Her dad's a famous sculptor.'

'Really?' said Carlo. 'Hey, that's amazing. It's one of the things . . .' He stopped speaking to press and squeeze the Snow Lady's nose into a more aristocratic shape. 'Sorry . . . I mean, sculpture is something I'd like to do. When I go to Art School.'

'Take no notice, Marianne,' said Laurie. 'He's just showing off. This is the first whisper I've heard about Art School. I thought . . .' He went up to Carlo. '. . . that we were going to set some Literature department on fire together somewhere.'

'I can't help being so creative,' said Carlo. 'Art School has just occurred to me. This is so great . . .' He gestured with one arm, 'All this white just lying there and we've made it into something.' He patted the Snow Lady on the arm. 'I mean someone. Ellie, you've been brilliant. Well done!'

48

'That's OK,' said Ellie, blushing.

'Is your dad really a famous sculptor?' Carlo wanted to know.

'He's not famous . . . not yet,' said Ellie. 'But he is a sculptor. I used to help him, but he's in America now.'

She wanted to say: 'It's one of the things I miss. He used to give me stone to chip at and wood to carve. I liked sitting in the corner of his studio and watching him.'

Instead she said: 'He had this massive warehouse place to do his work in. It was always cold there, even in summer. He made these huge figures out of wood and stone. He had to climb up ladders to do them. He told me something once . . .'

'What?' Carlo asked. 'Tell me.'

'Michelangelo said it and my dad believes it . . . He says the shape . . . the person . . . the thing, whatever he's making, is already in the stone, and he just has to chip away until he sort of . . . well . . . uncovers it, I suppose.'

'I believe it too,' said Carlo. 'I think he's right. She,' he stroked the fall of the Snow Lady's hair, 'has certainly been in the snow all along.'

Marianne began to chant and do a kind of War Dance.

'Garbage!' she cried. 'Garbage! Piffle! Nonsense! Rot! It's just a bunch of snowballs that you've squashed together. It only became a Lady because it was a bit lumpy at the front . . . you're both POTTY!'

'Time for my dear sister,' said Laurie soothingly, 'to withdraw. The cold is making her sour. She is developing splinters in her heart, like those kids in the Snow Queen story.'

'I'm off, don't worry,' said Marianne. 'I have to do a few

more things to the tree and then I'm going to have a bath. Hot, hot, hot. With bubbles. I'm going to make hot chocolate. I'm going to toast crumpets in front of the fire. I shall think of you all turning blue.'

'Hang on a mo, Marianne,' said Laurie. 'Before you do all that – and only because you've said you're going in anyway – will you go and find her something to wear? Please? Dearest, beloved sister?'

'OK,' said Marianne. 'I'll have a look through the dressing-up box if you like, only I'm not coming out again. I'll leave the stuff by the kitchen door. I might feel more sympathetic to this creature once I'm warm again.' She flicked her fingers in the direction of the Snow Lady and began to trudge up the slope towards the house.

'Don't be long,' Laurie shouted. 'It'll be dark soon.'

'Ten minutes.' Marianne's voice came to them even though she'd disappeared.

'What sort of things,' Carlo asked, 'are in your dressing-up box?'

He imagined cowboy hats, nurses' outfits, old pirate costumes, and rayon scarves that had seen better days.

'Wait and see,' said Ellie. 'She's finished now, isn't she?'

'Yes,' said Carlo. 'She's . . . awesome.'

They'd built her in exactly the right place, standing beside the gazebo, looking in at one of the windows. She had long, wide skirts. Two snowballs, shaped and smoothed and covered with more snow, became her bustle, and Ellie had scraped away at the bulk of her body to give her arms, and even hands. Carlo had fashioned the face, very carefully. You could make out eye sockets, a hawklike nose, and a mouth. He had pressed the snow, like plasticine. Laurie had

50

been allowed to work on the skirt, taking orders from Ellie and Carlo, and felt quite proud of what he'd managed to achieve. Behind the Snow Lady, the apricot sun looked like a lamp seen through fogged glass and the trees and shrubs beside the Lake were black against the blueish snow.

'Clothes!' Marianne's voice floated down from the house.

'Thanks!' cried Carlo and Ellie and Laurie, and they ran up to fetch them.

'Oh!' said Ellie, as she took a long, silver cloak out of the box. 'I remember this. It's the Queen of the Night cloak. How wonderful!'

'Who's the Queen of the Night?'

'She's a character from an opera . . . *The Magic Flute*,' said Laurie. 'Not a frightfully nice person, but a snappy dresser.'

'Perfect,' said Carlo. He'd found a battered three-cornered hat that was once velvet. 'Love the feather!'

It was Laurie who discovered the muff, and laughed.

'Marianne feels sorry for her,' he said. 'Can't bear her to be cold.'

They dressed the Snow Lady.

'She looks like a Princess now,' said Ellie. 'The gazebo is her palace.'

'Come on,' said Carlo, taking her by the hand and smiling at her. 'It's getting very dark now. Definitely time for hot chocolate.'

Ellie thought: I wish we could stay out here some more. When we get in, he'll let go of my hand. He's only being friendly. It doesn't mean anything. He thinks I'm a child, not like Marianne. I told him the story of the Lake ghosts while we were making the Lady, but I know his mind was somewhere else while I was talking. Soon, he'll stop thinking about me and think about her again. At the kitchen door, sure enough, Carlo and Laurie pushed ahead of her and into the warmth. She looked down towards the gazebo as she took off her wellingtons.

The Queen of the Night's silver cloak shimmered in the last of the daylight. Ellie thought she looked sad. Grow up, she said to herself as she took her gloves off. It's just a lump of snow in some old dressing-up clothes.

Work Rota: Ellie and Marianne

'Which would you rather,' said Ellie, as she walked round the table setting out the forks. 'Would you rather be amazingly fit and sprightly in your body and a bit . . . well, gone in the head, or the other way round? Have all your marbles and not be able to walk or look after yourself or anything?'

Marianne was folding napkins. She said: 'Definitely a healthy body.'

'Why?'

'Because if I was a bit soft in the head, I wouldn't know much. About how badly off I was, I mean. But just imagine being ill or in pain or not being able to move, or falling to bits generally, and realizing how awful things were for you. What's brought this on?'

'I was watching the Maestro . . . these are the right glasses, aren't they? . . . and he'd wandered out into the snow. He didn't even have a coat on. He was talking to our Snow Lady. I brought him in, but he didn't want to come. Not really. He thought it was Irene. He was talking to her. It was dead sad.'

'Poor old Maestro,' said Marianne, but Ellie knew she

wasn't really thinking about him when she went on to say, without even pausing: 'How many table mats do you think we need?'

'I don't know,' said Ellie. She went to fetch the salt and pepper set from the sideboard, but the thought of the Maestro with his arm around the Snow Lady filled her head. His slippers had been wet through. She sighed and hoped that Nana had made him change his socks.

8.00 p.m. The Dining Room

'Do you realize,' Laurie leaned across the table and said to Carlo, keeping his voice down so that none of the others would hear him, 'that all anyone has talked about for this whole meal has been a tiny little baby?'

Carlo was finishing the last of Nana's potatoes.

'These are the best spuds I've ever had, but I refuse to talk about potatoes. Say something important or interesting. Go on.'

Laurie smiled and said nothing. Meanwhile, Ellie, who was sitting beside Carlo, began to chat to him and he to her, and Laurie stopped trying to think of something thrilling to say to his friend. Instead, everything he wished he *could* say to Carlo came into his mind, like: I love the shape your shirt makes on your back, and when are we going to talk, properly talk, just the two of us without anyone there at all, and I want to show you the gazebo and what did you and Marianne say to one another while you were up in the attic, and (most important of all) am I ever going to be brave enough to whisper even a single word about how I feel about you?

Laurie sighed and helped himself to the crumble and an

53

almond biscuit. He tried to think of girls. There were some he admired and some he really liked, but not one of them had taken over his dreams nor made him tongue-tied and physically . . . what was the proper word? . . . *shaken*, as Carlo had. He looked around at his family. What would they say if they knew? Irene, who had spent years and years in the theatre . . . if he told her he was in love with Carlo, surely she wouldn't bat an eyelid?

Thinking the words, even to himself, made Laurie blush. He noticed Marianne, sitting next to Edmund further up the table, looking at him. She was smiling, so he smiled back. He said to himself: I bet she knows. I bet she knows everything. Then something else occurred to him. If she does know, what will she do? If Carlo went after her seriously, would she even spare a thought for her brother? Laurie doubted it and felt a sort of gloom fill his heart. Marianne, much as he adored her, couldn't exactly be described as selfless. Doing stuff for other people wasn't her style at all.

'So that's settled then,' came Irene's voice from the top of the table. 'Carrie will undertake the night feeds. We'll take the carrycot and Olivia's things upstairs after dinner. Really,' she smiled at Edmund, 'it's quite extraordinary, isn't it, that such a tiny creature should require so much elaborate . . .' She paused to find the right word and also to make sure that all eyes were upon her. '*Paraphernalia*.'

Everyone nodded and smiled and said yes, wasn't it amazing. Only Ellie was frowning so darkly that Carlo noticed and said: 'What's the matter? What did she say that upset you?'

'*I* should be looking after that baby. She knows me. I've

been with her more than anyone else in the family. Honestly, it's not fair . . . saying I'm too young. As if that matters. Carrie wouldn't know which end of a baby was which. I mean, can you imagine her changing a nappy?'

'I don't wish to imagine such a thing,' said Laurie. 'Not while I'm eating, thank you very much. And, anyhow, how good would *you* be at that? You'd never been near a baby till Olivia pitched up, isn't that right?'

'But I know,' said Ellie, 'that I'd be very good at it. I've watched Nana and I bet I'd be brilliant. I'm interested in babies and Carrie isn't. She's interested in . . . well, not babies anyway. Just because she . . .' Ellie was suddenly silent.

'She what?' said Laurie.

'I'm not saying,' Ellie said.

'Bet I know, anyway,' Laurie grinned at her.

'Maybe you do, but I'm not going to talk about it now, so there. Carrie might hear us.'

'No, she won't,' said Laurie. 'She and Edmund are communing.'

Carlo laughed. 'You mean they're talking. You always say things in a really strange way, d'you know that?'

'I strive,' said Laurie, 'for accuracy and felicity of expression. Nothing wrong with that, is there?'

Irene stood up as he was speaking.

'Coffee in the Library tonight, everyone. The tree's in the Chinese Lounge, and we can't see that yet, as you know,' she said, and swept out of the room. The others followed. Laurie watched Carlo making sure he went out of the door at the same time as Marianne. He smiled. All through dinner, *he'd* been planning to leave the room with Carlo,

55

calculating that then they'd probably end up sitting next to one another for coffee. Ho hum, he said to himself. Another daydream bites the dust. As he left, he turned out the lights.

10.00 p.m. The Dining Room
Pamina had watched them clearing the table. When the last dish had gone, when the last crumb had been swept up and the room was dark again, she found a place under one of the sideboards and wondered whether it would suit her purposes. No, she decided in the end. It was too cramped and, anyway, the people would soon return. After a short sleep, she would try to find somewhere else.

Whiteness has buried the road that links the village to the world and frozen crystals cling to telephone wires. Hardly anyone wants to move around in such a landscape, but those who do wade through the deep snow on foot, leaving a trail of dark holes behind them.

Midnight. The Garret Room
The Maestro looked out of the window. She was still there, looking into the gazebo. That cloak should have been hung up in Wardrobe, ready for tomorrow night's performance. If only she would return to her dressing room and change, he thought, then we could go and drink coffee at Chez Martine and I would have a cherry slice with whipped cream and Irene wouldn't eat anything, except for a small corner of my cake . . . she always likes just a taste.

The Maestro blinked. No, that wasn't Irene. Ellie had told him what it was. A Snow Woman, dressed in the silver cloak Irene had worn for *The Magic Flute*. The children had made it. Concentrate, Frederick. Do not let your thoughts run away with you. He drew the curtains shut and went to sit on the bed, trying to remember what his next task was. Pyjamas, he thought triumphantly. I must get into my pyjamas.

24 DECEMBER

12.45 a.m. The Conservatory

Somebody is crying, Ellie thought sleepily. I bet it's Olivia.

She sat up in bed and listened. Total silence. No, there it was again. It didn't sound like the baby. She's only been in the house for a few hours, but already I know so many of her cries. I can tell the difference between her 'give me some milk' sounds and her 'change my nappy' sounds. I know what she looks like when she's asleep, because I've watched her. No one really looks at babies, Ellie thought. Not properly. They can't speak, but you can tell what they want from how they move and from the noises they make. They should have put her in here with me. I wouldn't mind walking around with her in my arms. I'd do it all night if I had to. There was that noise again. Where was it coming from? Ellie got out of bed and remembered to put on her slippers.

Outside her bedroom door the corridor was long and dimly lit and she could see one staircase winding down into the dark, and another at the other end of the corridor leading up to where Carlo and Laurie were sleeping. And the Maestro, of course. He'd once told Ellie that he never slept at all, but when Ellie asked Nana about it, she'd made a sucking noise with her teeth and said he was a silly old man who didn't know if he was coming or going. There it was again – the noise – and it was definitely coming from downstairs.

Ellie shivered. Maybe she should wake Irene up, in case it was a burglar. How could it be a burglar, though? There was all that snow on the ground, and even the silliest thief in the world knew that meant footprints. Also, the Golden House had a sensitive alarm system. You only had to lean on a window from outside when it was on and that set it going. All the doors downstairs were left open so that Pamina could wander in and out. Could that sound possibly be her? Ellie tiptoed through the dark rooms. I don't believe in monsters hiding in the dark, she said to herself. This is the best place, the best house in the whole world, and no one in it wishes me any harm. If someone is crying, then I want to help them. No one should be miserable at Christmas, and it's already Christmas Eve.

Ellie stepped into the Conservatory, which was crowded with plants. They spilled over the rims of enormous china urns, and they fell out of baskets hanging from the glass ceiling. In the summer, you could see the blue sky, but now snow blocked out the light during the day and you could pretend you were in an igloo. There were rattan armchairs in the Conservatory, full of soft puffy cushions.

'Pamina?' Ellie whispered into the darkness. 'Is that you? Come here, kitty . . .'

Then she had a brilliant idea. Why on earth had she not thought of it before? She could have turned on some lights ages ago. She touched the switch and the sudden bright greenness of all the leaves dazzled her. She looked and then sat down very suddenly on the nearest chair, with all the breath knocked out of her body.

'Mum?' she breathed. 'Mum? Is it you crying? Oh, Mum, tell me what the matter is . . . why are you hiding down here?'

Whatever it was she had expected as an answer would have been less dreadful than what happened. Instead of saying something mother-ish, like what are you doing out of bed, or even, how dare you spy on me, Susanna bent her head down until it almost touched her knees, and began to wail as if she never intended to stop.

'I'll go and get Irene . . .' Ellie said, frightened. She stood up.

'No,' said Susanna. 'No, please. Don't get anyone. I'm OK. I'll stop. I promise. Just . . . just wait.'

'Is it Dad?' Ellie said. 'Has something happened to Dad?'

Susanna looked up, suddenly angry in the midst of her tears.

'No, it isn't,' she said. 'Why does everything always have to be about him? Why do you think of him first? Answer that!' She was almost spitting, and Ellie flinched.

'It doesn't . . . it isn't . . .' she said. 'It's just . . .'

'What?'

'Well, he hasn't phoned, and my present hasn't come yet . . . and I just wondered if—'

'You can stop wondering, then. The reason your present hasn't got here is because he's behaving true to form and he's left it too late for posting, that's all. That's if he hasn't forgotten all about getting you one, but then he's an artist, you know, and we must all make special allowances because nothing must ever be allowed to interfere with the Sacred Creative Process, and on and on and on until I'm sick of the sound of all the clichés.' She paused for breath, so Ellie spoke quickly, trying to sound as if she really believed what she was saying; trying to sound tough.

'That's not true, Mum. He would never forget me, or my present. I know he wouldn't. It's probably,' she changed her tone to a soothing one, hoping to calm Susanna down a little, 'sitting in a post office somewhere and they can't deliver it because of all the snow. Dad loves me. I know he does.'

Susanna was obviously all cried out. She took a tissue out of her dressing-gown pocket and began to blow her nose vigorously and wipe her eyes. Ellie looked at her and was filled with despair. Was it true? Could Dad have forgotten all about her? It was easy to say you loved someone, but what if you then leave them and go away right to the other side of the world? Doesn't that mean your love's a bit . . . well . . . feeble? And it could get less, couldn't it? Your picture of someone far away went on fading and fading and it was quite hard even to remember what they looked like.

Ellie spent hours sometimes poring over the photos, but

61

they weren't the real thing. And the real thing, she admitted to herself when she was being truly honest, was vanishing from her mind, so that it was an effort even to recall what he sounded like, or some of the funny things he said.

She felt tears of longing and misery prickle behind her eyelids as Susanna stood up, and said: 'Right. Well. We'd best be off to bed now, I suppose. Tomorrow . . . I mean today, is Christmas Eve and we'll need every ounce of our energy, I'm quite sure.'

'No,' said Ellie. 'You *can't* go to bed like that. You just can't.'

'Why not? I'll be OK now, I promise. It all . . . well, it all got a bit much, that's all.'

Ellie wanted to shake her mother. Why was she so irritating? Couldn't she see?

'You may be OK,' she said gently, 'but I'm not. I want to know what it is. I've known for days that you aren't fine at all, even though you keep saying you are. Tell me. Tell me what's the matter. Go on. Sit down. Just say everything. Everything you have to say to get it off your chest.'

'Your father always advised getting things off his chest, didn't he?' Susanna sat down on one of the puffy chairs and sighed. 'I'm sorry I was nasty about him. Of course he loves you and of course he's sent you a present. He never was too well organized about dates and things, though, so you mustn't mind if it's late.'

'I won't,' said Ellie. 'Don't worry, but don't change the subject. It's *you* I'm worried about. It's you I'm always worried about. Oh God, Mum, please don't start crying again! What have I said?'

'Nothing. I'm sorry,' Susanna scrubbed frantically at her nose. 'I'll stop now. Look.' She sniffed.

Ellie said: 'What happened?'

'I met a man,' Susanna began and stopped. Then she went on. 'I thought he was lovely at first . . . you know, handsome and kind and everything, and he seemed to like me, but . . .'

'But what?'

'He wasn't. Nice. He was . . . he turned out to be quite horrible really.'

Ellie relaxed. 'Was he married? Is that what was wrong with him?'

'That was one thing, yes. But not the main thing. How did you know that?'

'I guessed, that's all. What was the main thing that *was* wrong with him?'

'I hate him. I hate him for what he's made me do. I hate him because of what he's done to me. He's turned me into someone I'm not, and I'll never forgive him. Actually, I don't hate him.'

'No?' Ellie looked at her mother. I love her, she thought. I love her better than anyone in the world, so why do I want to hit her? What's the matter with her? Or is it something wrong with me that makes me feel so furious with her so much of the time?

'Who?' she said, struggling not to let the anger show in her voice. 'Who *do* you hate?'

'I hate myself,' Susanna said, and her daughter burst out:

'Don't be ridiculous! That's a stupid thing to say. Why should you hate yourself? You haven't done anything so terrible. Lots of people fall in love with the wrong person. It happens all the time.'

Susanna laughed. 'So worldly-wise and only thirteen,' she said.

A red mist of fury filled Ellie's head. She hissed: 'Stop it! Stop being patronizing. It's not *my* fault I'm thirteen. That's got nothing to do with anything. You never speak to me properly, not ever. I'm just supposed to *guess* what's happening to you. You're selfish and irritating and silly and the divorce is all your fault and I'm not surprised Dad couldn't stand living with you!' As soon as the words were out of her mouth, Ellie regretted them and because she couldn't unsay them, she burst into tears and sat down and covered her face with her hands.

'You're as bad as me,' Susanna said, hugging Ellie. 'We could solve the water shortage between the two of us, no problem, eh? Stop crying, lovey. Don't be sad. I know you didn't mean all that . . . look at me, it's OK. Come on. Smile.'

Ellie risked a glance at her mother, and said: 'I haven't brought a hankie.'

'Ah, well,' said Susanna. 'I'm a better crier in the middle of the night than you, then. I made sure to bring a packet of tissues. Here.'

'You came prepared,' Ellie said. 'Did you know you were going to cry?'

'I've been wanting to weep for days, only I didn't want you to catch me, and then we came down here where everyone simply has to know everyone else's business and, well, the middle of the night in the Conservatory seemed like a good bet, till you appeared. Do you want to come to my room? I'll make you a cup of cocoa or something.'

'In a minute,' Ellie said. 'First, I want to know why you hate yourself. Is it because you feel silly going off with that bloke?'

'No, not really.' Susanna looked up. 'It's much worse than that.'

'Never mind,' said Ellie. 'Tell me.'

'You'll hate me. You'll never forgive me. I find it hard to forgive myself.'

'I won't hate you.'

'Promise?'

'Yes.'

'OK.' Susanna looked down at the tiled floor. Then she looked up and Ellie could see that her eyes were full of tears. 'I had an abortion. That's it.'

Ellie said nothing. All at once, she felt as though every drop of blood in her body had turned to ice. She tried to think of something to say, but her head was empty: completely white and cold and with not a single thought in it anywhere. Susanna spoke into the silence:

'You can't begin to imagine, Ellie, how awful I feel. How awful everything was. Oh, I don't mean the operation. That was ... well ... as OK as that sort of thing ever is. You remember ... I said I was going to a conference, and you went to stay with Helen. I was in a lovely clinic for two days, and all the doctors and nurses couldn't have been kinder, but I felt ill ... I just felt sick with guilt and fear and, oh, all sorts of things.'

'I thought,' Ellie spoke slowly and the words seemed to

her to come from somewhere black at the bottom of a kind of well in her heart, 'that you were against abortion.'

'I was. I am. Only . . .'

'Only what?'

'I couldn't bear it. The thought of that man's baby growing and growing inside me was so dreadful. Don't you understand? Just the idea of it filled me with horror. I could never, ever have loved the child. I wanted to be rid of it, and of myself too. I was disgusted. I would have done it . . . I'd have killed myself, but of course I couldn't, because of you.'

'It was a baby,' said Elliè. 'How could you murder a baby?'

'It wasn't a baby,' Susanna said gently. 'It was a very, very new foetus. Less than twelve weeks old. Don't think of it as a baby.'

Ellie stood up and walked stiffly to the door.

'I'm going to bed now,' she said. 'Goodnight.'

'Ellie, don't go yet. Say something, Ellie. Please.'

'There's nothing I *can* say,' said Ellie. 'I feel sick.'

She walked through the sleeping house, up the stairs, along the corridor and into her room. When she got there, she got into bed and stared at the ceiling. She knows, Ellie thought. Of course she knows. She's always known that I've wanted a brother or a sister, more than anything. I'll never, ever forgive her. She felt the tears slide sideways down her cheeks, wetting both sides of her neck. I don't care, she thought. I don't care if this bed gets sopping wet. I'll never be happy again.

2.00 a.m. The Basement Flat

There was a time, Nana thought, and not so long ago at that, when there wouldn't have been any question of where that baby would sleep. She would have been here, at my side. But, she supposed, they were right and she *was* too old to be getting up at all hours to warm bottles and change nappies and walk the floor with a little creature who was missing her mother. I'm awake now, of course, she said to herself, but it's not the same. I can lie and look at the ceiling, and then I can turn round and look at the wall, and if the worst comes to the worst, I can always make myself a cup of tea. I wouldn't really like to have the responsibility for little Olivia.

Nana wished, not for the first time, that the children still hung up their stockings. Being Father Christmas, tiptoeing from bed to bed in the middle of the night and leaving tangerines and nuts and little almond biscuits made from the recipe given to her by a Viennese pastry-cook whose name she'd long ago forgotten . . . oh, that was fun! Irene decided they were too old for such things when Laurie was ten, without considering that Ellie, at least, was still a child. And everyone knew that what Irene decided stayed decided forever. She, Nana, had retaliated by starting another tra-dition, and for the last few years, she'd been in the habit of placing a small basket next to each child's plate on Christmas morning, containing the same treats she used to enjoy putting in the stockings.

In the kitchen, everything was ready. She'd been pre-paring for so long that there was really very little that still had to be done. Only last-minute things. It was a pity about the snow. Would it stop people coming to the Midnight

Service? She wouldn't dare venture out in it, not even just down as far as the church. She would miss Irene's carol. When did that begin? Years and years ago. Every Christmas, Irene chose a carol and sang it, without telling anyone but the organist what it was going to be. Silence filled the church and her voice, *that voice*, like a glorious bird that had been caged all year, was set free; let out for the whole of the village to admire. Naturally, everyone knew who she was, but they didn't make a fuss about it. Still, the Midnight Service was always packed, and for a few weeks after Christmas every year, all the staff, and also anyone from the village who visited the house mentioned it; and sighed to themselves when they remembered how beautiful it had been.

4.45 a.m. The White Room

'Carrie? Are you awake?' Susanna put her head round the door of the White Room. 'I knew you would be . . . I heard Olivia crying.'

'I'm so sorry,' said Carrie. 'I didn't realize you could hear her from your room. I can't imagine why babies keep these awful hours. A design fault on the part of the Creator . . . that's what Laurie said tonight.'

'It's not the baby. I was awake anyway.'

Carrie looked at her sister. She thought of all sorts of things to say, to ask, such as: why do you look so awful? Why are you awake when you're well known in the family for sleeping through everything and being impossible to get out of bed in the morning? Why haven't you spoken to me properly since you came to the Golden House when we've always told one another everything?

68

Instead, she said, as lightly as she could: 'Just let me put this little creature back in her cot, and then I'll make you a cup of peppermint tea.'

Susanna laughed. 'Peppermint tea! I could do with a double vodka. You think peppermint tea is the elixir of life.'

'It's very comforting,' said Carrie, 'and good for the digestion. I've even got some of Nana's mince pies in a tin somewhere. They're impossible to escape. We can have a *nessun dorma*.'

Nessun dorma . . . none shall sleep. Susanna had practically forgotten their childish term for sleepless nights, hers and Letta's and Carrie's. It was, of course, the name of an aria from *Turandot*. When they were children, they often speculated about why their mother loved singing the title role so much, when Turandot was such a cruel and icy-hearted princess.

'It's the costume,' said Letta. It was true that the white brocade gown scattered with pearls and the tall headdress that looked as though it was carved out of ivory were beautiful. They suited Irene's dark eyes and made her appear taller than she really was.

'I think she likes knowing things other people don't know,' Susanna used to say, because the story was about a riddle. Anyone who wanted to marry Turandot had to guess at the answer, and if they didn't guess correctly, they were put to death. 'And she likes bossing people about.'

'I think', Carrie said, and her sisters never paid much attention to her because she was the youngest, 'she likes the falling in love bit at the end.'

Now Susanna thought that her mother had probably

enjoyed the part for a combination of all the reasons they'd thought of as children, and also for the wonderful music.

'Letta's not here,' she said to Carrie, 'so it's not a proper *nessun dorma*, and anyway the night is nearly over, even though I haven't been asleep.'

'Not been asleep!' Carrie was shocked. 'Where have you been? What have you been doing?'

'Confessing.'

'Come on, Susanna. Stop being enigmatic. You know I'm going to say – confessing what? So why don't you just sit down over there and tell me everything. I can see you're not OK.'

'I had a row with Ellie. Well, not a row exactly. She was furious. She will never, I think, forgive me.'

'How melodramatic!' said Carrie. 'What on earth have you done?'

'I had an abortion. About three weeks ago.'

Carrie was silent for such a long time, that Susanna went on: 'There's nothing you can really say, is there? I told Ellie all about it. I know she wants a brother or sister more than anything, but I had to do it. She couldn't understand why. She would have looked after it. I wouldn't have had to bother myself with the child hardly at all.'

'I thought,' Carrie said at last, 'that you were against abortion.'

'I was. It's easy to say you are until you find that you can't bear it . . . can't even think of what it is . . . only know you want it gone. I didn't know it would hurt so much. Not physically, but here.' She touched her breast. 'It hurts here. Like Turandot, really . . . my heart feels as if it's made of ice. And part of the pain is about Ellie. Is she ever going to forgive me?'

'You shouldn't underestimate her,' said Carrie. 'She's very grown up in many ways. She'll understand your feelings in the end.'

Susanna nodded and sighed.

'But she loves Christmas so much and I've spoiled it for her. I should have waited and told her at home.'

'No, you were right to tell her here,' Carrie said. 'Then she can talk about it to someone . . . Marianne, perhaps.'

'Oh, heavens, the whole family will know. I can't bear it.'

'They *will* know,' Carrie said. 'You must have realized you couldn't keep something like that to yourself. It's because we love one another that we want to know everything. It's not just nosiness.'

'I must sleep.' Susanna yawned. 'Do I dare go to bed now and miss breakfast?'

As far as Irene was concerned, being at Death's Door was the only excuse for missing breakfast.

'Yes,' Carrie said. 'I'll make up some story, don't worry.'

'Thank you,' said Susanna, and flung her arms around Carrie, thinking: I love her so much and yet I can't remember when I last hugged her. 'You're a good person to talk to.'

'Go to bed,' said Carrie. 'Sleep. Sleep for a long time.'

While almost everyone slept, the cold made lace patterns on the windows, and turned soft drifts into solid masses, like land-bound icebergs. The silver fabric of the Snow Lady's cloak had become as stiff as metal.

9.00 a.m. The Dining Room

Irene sounded distinctly frosty at breakfast as she peered down the table and asked: 'What's become of Ellie? And where is Susanna?'

Carrie began to tell a story of Ellie being sick in the night and having a late lie in, and Susanna being up all night to attend to her. Marianne could see at once that the whole thing was a lie from start to finish. If Derek hadn't distracted everyone with his pronouncement just at that moment, Irene wouldn't have been taken in for a second.

'I've been listening to the local radio station,' he said, spreading Nana's home-made marmalade right to the very edges of his toast, and addressing the whole table in what Marianne thought of as his typical schoolteacher's manner, 'and I'm reliably informed that there will be no break in the weather for the foreseeable future.'

Marianne suddenly understood the true meaning of words she'd read in books a thousand times. Her heart sank. It really did. She could feel something plunging like a stone from a place almost in her throat to somewhere right down in her stomach.

'What,' she asked as soon as she felt able to speak, 'does that mean?'

'The roads are impassable, I'm afraid,' Derek said, 'unless there's some kind of a thaw. We are, as it were, marooned on a desert island.' He looked at Letta (who, Marianne noticed, had turned very pale), and showed his teeth. He wasn't smiling. Not properly. Briefly, she wondered whether this had anything to do with the bickering Laurie had overheard in the kitchen yesterday, but she was too unhappy to worry about anything other than her own predicament.

She had to phone Andy. How could she do that without any of the others hearing? Her fantasies of the all-night disco at La Bodega were no better than mirages. And someone would make sure Andy wasn't on his own for long, Marianne had no doubt of that. For a second her misery gave way to anger and she felt like picking up all Irene's twinkling pieces of flower-patterned, gold-rimmed china and smashing them into the carpet under the heel of her shoe.

'What's the matter?' said Carlo.

'Nothing,' Marianne answered, sullen and not looking at him.

'Something *is* wrong,' Carlo persisted. 'You're grinding your teeth.'

'It's none of your business', she hissed at him, 'what I do with my own teeth.'

Across the table she saw Laurie raise his eyebrows and smirk at Carlo, and she turned the full force of her rage on him.

'What're you making faces at?' she said. 'Everyone knows that *you're* thrilled we're all going to be stuck here for centuries, though they don't know why, do they? Not like me. I know. Shall I say?'

'Shut up, Marianne,' said Laurie and his face was scarlet.

'Children,' said Irene from the top of the table, 'you are behaving like infants. What is going on? Why are you all so quarrelsome? Stop this nonsense at once, please. It's Christmas Eve and there's plenty to be done. Marianne, darling, before you put the finishing touches to the tree, I'd be endlessly grateful if you went to see what's become of Ellie. I shall speak to Susanna myself when she appears.'

73

'Yes, of course,' said Marianne, and stood up to go. Laurie was looking so miserable that she took pity on him and leaned over his shoulder to whisper in his ear on her way out of the room.

'It's OK, Big Bro. I shan't say a word. Your secret's safe with me . . . my lips are sealed, and so forth.'

On her way upstairs, she wondered, not for the first time, whether Laurie *knew*. She and Stacey had decided long ago that he was probably gay, but did he admit it to himself? And if he did, how keen was he on Carlo? And can't he see that Carlo is after me? And if he can, does he mind? They'd discussed it all last year, when Stacey developed a crush on Laurie. He'd shown not the slightest bit of interest in her.

'Which needn't,' Stacey said, 'necessarily mean anything, because it could just be me he didn't fancy, but have you ever seen him anywhere near a girl?'

Marianne had to confess that, no, girls didn't figure much in her brother's life.

'But he's nearly seventeen and he's so cute,' Stacey said.

'Cute?'

'Yes, cute. That's what makes me sure. Why don't you ask him?'

'What, just flat out, like that: are you gay?'

'Yes. Why not?'

'He might not want anyone to know,' Marianne said.

'That's ridiculous,' said Stacey. 'There's nothing wrong with being gay.'

'Well, I know that, and you know that,' Marianne said, 'but Laurie might feel embarrassed about it. Boys are a bit strange about stuff like that. He might not want to talk about it.'

74

'But you're his sister,' Stacey said. 'I thought brothers and sisters told one another everything.'

'That's because you're an only child,' Marianne said, 'so you don't know what you're talking about.'

'Oh, I give up,' said Stacey, and she had. She'd turned her attention to Simon Dukes, and Marianne was left to observe Laurie on her own.

Outside the Blue Room, she stopped thinking about her brother and began to wonder about Ellie. She knelt down.

'Ellie?' She looked through the keyhole, but all she could see was a corner of the bed and a bit of curtain. 'Ellie, it's me. Open up. Come on.'

She rattled the doorknob around, but her cousin had obviously decided to lock herself in.

'Ellie, please, I need to talk to you. You'll never guess what Dad told us this morning . . . honestly, Ellie, I'm in such a state about it and I *have* to talk to someone. I don't know what to do. Open the door. I want to tell you a secret. Actually, two secrets. No, three.'

What the hell, Marianne said to herself. Ellie won't tell anyone else, and I have to do something. And what's more, it's working.

She stood up as the door opened slowly.

'Ellie!' she said, when she saw her cousin's face. 'Oh, Ellie, love, tell me what's happened.'

Ellie made a whimpering sound and flung herself into Marianne's arms.

'There, there,' said Marianne, as soothingly as she could. 'Calm down and tell me all about it.' She tried very hard not to think about salty tears getting on her new light-blue sweatshirt and leaving marks.

11.30 a.m. The Garden

Carrie and Edmund were making their way back to the Golden House. They had been to see that everything was in order for Mr Teasland to take over at the Surgery.

'I can't remember ever having worn so many clothes before,' said Carrie, and her breath curled in white streamers in front of her face. 'Nana knitted this scarf for me when I was twelve. And these wellingtons! It's years and years since I've worn wellingtons.'

'I wear them all the time,' said Edmund. 'I wouldn't be without them for the world. How do you manage? Don't your feet get dreadfully wet?'

'I don't go out very much,' said Carrie, 'and hardly ever if it's raining.'

How could she explain to Edmund, when she had never really been able to explain it to herself? Whenever she left the Golden House, the minute she stepped outside, suddenly she found it harder and harder to breathe. The sky, which to everyone seemed high, high up, began to weigh on her and she had the sensation of something pressing her down. The space all around made her feel dizzy. Irene had the gazebo put up mainly for her, because she'd asked for somewhere in the garden which would be like a house. She went down to the shop in the village from time to time, but train travel or road travel terrified her and she avoided it as much as she could.

'It was very kind of you,' Edmund went on, 'to come down with me.'

'I like,' said Carrie, 'seeing what animals are coming to consult you. I always meet someone I know.'

'I should think you know every dog for miles around.'

He sighed, and fell silent. They walked along slowly. Every step in the snow, Carrie thought, is an effort, but how lovely to have Edmund all to herself for a while.

One of the main drawbacks of living in a big family was hardly ever being able to be alone with just one other person. Last night, with Susanna ... well, early this morning ... was so strange. She remembered that, as a small child, she could never talk to *just* one of her sisters without the other joining in. It wasn't quite as bad now, of course. Susanna and Letta had left home long ago and, when she was on her own with Irene and Nana and the Maestro, she occasionally missed the crowded feeling the house took on at Christmas time.

But I've never, she thought, been alone with Edmund before. Serena, his wife, had always been standing next to him, or else she'd seen him at the Surgery when Pamina needed injections, or when he'd come up to the house for consultations with Irene on matters of Feline Welfare. Yesterday, she'd stood in front of him with a cup of coffee, to comfort him, and he'd looked at her, and his eyes had widened as though he were seeing her properly for the first time.

'You're very kind, Carrie,' he'd said, and his voice made the blood run in her veins like fire and she could feel herself blushing. Since then, he'd been in and out of her room to look at Olivia and they'd talked in a normal, friendly way. Then he'd thanked her for doing the night feed, and she'd murmured: 'It's a pleasure, really,' and he'd touched her briefly on the shoulder.

Now they were getting closer and closer to the house.

'The children,' said Edmund, 'have made a splendid job

of that Snow Lady, haven't they? She looks real, doesn't she?'

'Yes,' said Carrie, 'though I don't think they'd like being called children.'

'They'd hate it,' said Edmund. 'I'd never call them that to their faces. Carrie . . .' He paused.

'Yes?'

'Will you come to the service tonight? I always go. I know you sometimes stay away, but please come tonight. I'm sure Nana will babysit, just for once. I'd like you to be there.'

'I don't think I should leave Nana and the Maestro all on their own . . .' She hesitated.

'Carrie . . .' Edmund said, 'I don't know how to put this, but . . .' He looked up at the sky as though the words he was looking for might have been up there, hanging in the air. 'Well, I'm aware . . . I've been aware for a long time . . . of your feelings.' He took her hands, and said: 'Carrie, don't turn away like that. I can't feel your fingers through these thick gloves, but please, look at me.'

'I can't,' Carrie said. 'I don't want to . . .'

'Why not?'

'I'm embarrassed.'

'There's nothing, nothing in the world at all, to be embarrassed about. I wanted to say . . . well, of course, I'm still a married man technically, at least, but I wanted to tell you . . . oh, Carrie, this is ridiculous!'

He pulled her awkwardly towards him and kissed her. They clung together for a long moment, then broke apart and began to walk again in the direction of the house, their feet dragging in the heavy snow. Carrie looked down at the ground and heard a strange, humming sound filling her head. Her mouth where Edmund had kissed her felt warm, even in the icy air, and her heart . . . well, yes, it was – everything they said about fluttering hearts was true. Once, she'd caught a butterfly in her hands and it had moved its wings briefly against her fingers in the moment before she let it go. That was what her heart felt like, under the layers and layers of woolly garments: like a scarlet butterfly.

11.40 a.m. The Blue Room

Ellie always slept in the Blue Room, because blue was her favourite colour. And this year, she thought, it's a good colour to be in because everything is turning out so horrible. She nearly started crying all over again when she thought of all the different things that were swirling around in a mess in the middle of her head and making her miserable. It's not fair. That's what she'd told Marianne, and Marianne said: 'Life isn't fair, Ellie. It really is time you stopped thinking it was.'

She was right. Of course she was right and Ellie *did* know it. She also knew that she was a lucky person and, compared with children who were starving or beaten or abused or just plain neglected, there was obviously nothing wrong with her. But still. She felt miserable and that was that. She felt . . . disappointed. Christmas was something she looked forward to all year. She loved every single thing about it, and now her mother had spoiled it. Whatever Marianne said, whatever anyone said, Ellie felt as though she'd lost a sister. And no one would expect me to be happy if a slightly *older sister* had died.

'But you must stop crying,' Marianne said. 'Crying

doesn't help. All it does is make your eyes sting and your face puff up and look red. As it is, I'm going to have to come and fix you up with concealers and things before you're fit to be seen.'

She'd told Ellie three secrets, thinking that they might cheer her up, but two of them made her feel even worse, and the third one was boring. She told her all about Letta coming back to the Golden House across the snow very early in the morning, and then lying about it. Ellie then remembered about the phone and how Letta had slammed it down the moment she knew someone was listening.

'That proves it,' Marianne said. 'She's up to something. Maybe she's having an affair.'

'But she's old,' Ellie made a face.

'She doesn't think so. And look at your mother . . .'

'Don't,' Ellie nearly started crying again. 'I don't want to think about it.'

The other secrets were more interesting. Marianne thought Laurie was gay. Ellie had never met any gay people, so she didn't know what she thought about them, although of course if what Marianne said was true, then she did . . . she knew Laurie very well, and he was her favourite person in the world, after her parents and Marianne. It didn't matter a bit, she decided. Who cares if you like men better than women or the other way around? She certainly didn't.

'Is Carlo gay too?' she asked Marianne.

'I don't think so,' Marianne said. 'Not judging by the way he's been coming on to me.'

'Has he?'

'Oh, yes. Though he could be bi, of course.'

'Do you fancy him?' Ellie asked.

'He's OK,' said Marianne. 'I'm not exactly discouraging him.'

So that was that. Ellie said nothing. She had vaguely heard of bisexuals – people who liked both men and women – but she didn't really understand how that worked and she was too embarrassed to ask Marianne, who would think she was a real baby. What she *did* know was that Carlo wasn't interested in her. He probably thought she was a baby too. That word! Why did it keep coming up everywhere? Ellie slammed the silver hairbrush down on the dressing table and peered at her red face in the mirror. Normally, when she was staying at the Golden House, one of the things she liked best was having such a posh dressing table. Now she wished she was in her own little room at home with a square of mirror stuck to the door of a cupboard that she never had to open if she knew she looked revolting.

Marianne's third secret was going to cause trouble. She'd made her mind up to leave school next year, straight after GCSEs, and go to drama school. She was going to concentrate on Modern Dance and Singing, and be a Musical Comedy Star.

'They'll flip their lids!' she told Ellie, looking rather excited at the prospect. 'All of them. Irene would be on my side if I had operatic ambitions, but, darling, musicals! How *low*, how *vulgar!*'

Ellie laughed. Marianne could mimic Irene exactly. And she was right about the ructions. Letta and Derek were parents who didn't believe in life without A levels, and then university. They would say, for instance, that her own ambition to go to art school was a bit of a waste of time:

OK for those who *couldn't* do anything else, but for a clever child who did well at exams . . . unthinkable.

She stood up and went to the window. That was another reason why she loved the Blue Room – you could see the whole garden. Who was that, down by the gazebo? Carrie and Edmund. They were standing very close together and . . . no, they couldn't be! Ellie pressed her nose against the glass, so that she could see better. They *were*. They were *kissing*. Properly, like people in a film.

That explains it, she thought. That's why Carrie wants to look after Olivia all the time. She's after Edmund. He hasn't exactly wasted time since his wife left. Sometimes Ellie thought grown-ups had no idea what morals were. But what a good secret to tell Marianne! She smiled. That was one good thing about being unhappy. Marianne had been so kind, much kinder than she normally was. She really seemed to care about me, Ellie thought. Perhaps she *is* fond of me, after all. She's going to help me do my face up later, with her own make-up.

In spite of everything, Ellie began to feel a little more cheerful. Being cross and miserable was such hard work, and continuing to hate Susanna would be impossible. I'll still never forgive her for what she did, but maybe I'm a bit more cheerful than I was, she thought. Maybe Christmas *will* be quite fun after all. She went to the chest of drawers, took out the presents she'd made and lined them up on the floor, ready for wrapping. Lots of lovely birds, which she'd made out of modelling clay that hardened magically before you painted it. There were owls and swans and eagles and robins and even a bluebird of happiness. That was for her mother.

1.00 p.m. The Kitchen

Pamina woke up from a lovely dream. This room was always full of good smells, and her sleeping thoughts had been of past plates of grilled fish and prawns and the thousand small treats that Nana always seemed to find for her.

Lately, she had lost her appetite and had no desire to eat real food, so she spent more and more time with her eyes closed, remembering it. The back door – the door to the garden – was closed now, but humans liked to come and go all the time and someone would open it later, almost certainly. Then, she would leave and look for a suitable spot. It was nearly time.

2.00 p.m. The Library

Carlo thought: maybe Irene's right, and I *am* still a child. He couldn't help the feelings of excitement that came over him when he thought of all the presents he'd be getting tomorrow. Seriously kid-like, that was. But all over the house they were wrapping. They made a Thing of it, this family, just as they made a Thing of all the rest of the Christmas stuff. He'd wrapped his presents before he'd left home, and couldn't help feeling smug at what everyone would say when they saw them. He'd spent ages after school in the Art Studio, shaping small, flat pieces of stained glass into apples and oranges. He'd made special, different things for Laurie and Marianne, and with all of them, if you hung them at the window, light shone through them and they looked brilliant.

He was at a loose end, no two ways about it, with no one to talk to, just slobbing around in the Library, pretending to read and actually daydreaming. When Irene came and found him, he was almost dozing. Doing nothing was exhausting.

'Carlo, dear,' she said, as he sprang up on the sofa into something like a sitting position. 'Did I wake you?'

'No, honestly, I was just—'

'I understand perfectly.' She smiled. 'It's the most tiring activity, isn't it, waiting and waiting for something to happen.'

Carlo nodded. What *did* she mean? What was going to happen?

'I mean Christmas, of course. We do make rather a *production* of it in this family, don't we? I hope it isn't all too much for you?'

'I'm having a really good time,' said Carlo. 'And I love this house.'

Irene sighed. 'It's beautiful, isn't it? I shall miss it dreadfully.'

'Are you going somewhere?'

'No, no, of course not . . . I don't know why I said such a thing. I suppose I might have meant once I'm dead . . . because, although of course I hope that's years and years away, I *am* much older than I look. At least, that's what I tell myself.'

'You don't look old at all,' Carlo said. He was used to saying such things. He said them to Bette all the time. She needed reassurance, and he knew it. He'd learned, long ago when he was really no more than a little boy, that when his mother said: 'Tell me *honestly* what you think about this dress/blouse/pair of shoes' what she meant was: 'Tell me how lovely I look.'

84

'Flatterer!' Irene said. 'Never mind. It does a person good to be told such lies, doesn't it?'

She was babbling. She wanted him to forget what she'd said, about missing the Golden House. What could she possibly have meant? He would ask Laurie, later.

Meanwhile, Irene was saying: 'I nearly forgot what I came in here to ask you, Carlo darling, but I've remembered now. It's a *huge* favour. Not on the Work Rota, but would you mind just running the Hoover along the upstairs corridor for me? I was going to ask Laurence, but he's up to his armpits in the most *garish* Christmas paper imaginable.'

'I'd love to,' said Carlo.

'You're a treasure,' said Irene. 'I'm so glad Laurence asked you to join us.'

'Me too.'

She glided towards the door.

'Thank you, my dear,' she said, and was gone, leaving behind her a fragrance like old roses.

Work Rota: Carlo

How typical of Irene, Carlo thought, to have an altogether classier vacuum cleaner than anyone else! It followed you on its smooth-running wheels, looking like a robot or a pet or something. Carlo was thinking about what Irene had said. What did it mean? He went on hoovering, and gradually his thoughts turned to Marianne. Where was she? It couldn't, surely, be taking her this long to do her presents? She'd spent half the morning locked up with Ellie, who'd been sick in the night or something. Laurie reckoned that wasn't true.

'She'll have had a row with Susanna,' he'd said. 'They're always getting at each other.'

Whatever, Carlo thought. There was no sign of Marianne anywhere. He pulled the Hoover along to the carpet just outside her room and turned the suction switch up to its highest (and noisiest) setting. It worked. After about five seconds, the door opened and Marianne yelled: '*Must* you? How am I meant to get any . . .' Her voice faded when she caught sight of Carlo and she blushed.

Carlo turned the machine off and said: 'I'm sorry, I had no idea . . . I thought you might still be with Ellie.'

'What on earth are you up to?'

'Irene asked me to hoover up here. She found me in the Library.'

'Oh, well, if it's Irene's orders, I suppose you'd better get on with it.'

'I've nearly finished,' Carlo said. 'Will you be coming downstairs soon?'

'No,' said Marianne. 'I've got to go and help the Maestro. He gets in a dreadful muddle with his presents. Carrie buys them for him, and Laurie and I take turns to help him parcel them up. It's a real drag. He never stops talking.'

'Can I come with you? I'll help. I'm good at wrapping. Please.'

She smiled. 'OK. A sucker for punishment, you are. See you in about half an hour.'

'Am I allowed to finish vacuuming this bit?' Carlo grinned.

'I suppose so. I shall be in the shower.'

She disappeared into her room. Carlo continued his progress along the corridor, his head full of visions of Marianne in the shower. Every word that Irene had said to him in the Library had vanished completely from his mind.

The snow had fallen on Wedderling in such a way that certain electricity lines were spared, and the Golden House was filled with light and warmth. The telephone lines, though, were down and there was nothing but deep, white silence on the line.

3.45 p.m. The Garret Room

'There, Maestro,' said Marianne. She and Carlo were sitting on the floor of the Garret Room, and between them was a pile of presents, all neatly wrapped in jolly paper dotted with beaming Santas and gormless-looking reindeer with bright-red noses.

'Thank you, my dears,' said the Maestro. 'Without you, who knows if I would do anything? Please take chocolates. Marianne, do you remember where they are?'

'Of course,' Marianne said. 'In the bottom drawer of the chest of drawers.'

Carlo had found it very hard to concentrate on the wrapping because there was so much to look at: framed photographs on every wall, which all seemed to be of Irene.

'You are admiring them, Alexei,' the Maestro said. Carlo had given up correcting this particular mistake.

'It's Irene, isn't it?' he said. 'She was very beautiful.'

'And with talent to match. Here, look; Irene as Violetta, Irene as Pamina, Irene as Mimi, and here as Turandot. Oh, she was the greatest Turandot of her generation. No doubt of that.'

'Is this you?' Carlo said, pointing to a tall and handsome man in full evening dress, standing next to Irene, who was nearly invisible behind an enormous bouquet of flowers tied up with satin ribbons. Those ribbons, Carlo realized, must have been in the box he saw yesterday.

'Yes,' said the Maestro. 'I find it hard to remember many things, but that I can recall as if it happened yesterday. Irene had just given a recital. The Festival Hall in nineteen fifty-eight, or fifty-nine . . . Strauss's *Four Last Songs*. So beautiful.'

He blinked. Was he about to burst into tears? Carlo looked at him and he was wiping his eyes with a hankie. He said: 'My eyes . . . they have begun to water, these last few years. Forgive me.'

'Here we are, Maestro,' said Marianne. 'Chocolates!'

'Excellent,' said the Maestro. 'Please find me a coffee cream, dear child.'

Marianne picked one out. 'Here you go,' she said, and held the box out to Carlo.

'Thanks,' he said. Then: 'Have you ever looked at this photo?'

'Of the Maestro and Irene in all their glory? I've had to admire it till I'm blue in the face.'

'The Maestro reminds me of someone.'

'Tell me about it!' Marianne laughed. 'Every time some hunk has his picture in the paper, Irene cuts it out and keeps it and tells us how like the Maestro this or that person is . . . Nigel Havers, he was one of them. And Charles Dance. They don't *really* look like him though, any of them.'

Carlo said: 'Never mind. It'll come to me.'

Marianne turned to the Maestro and said: 'We're going to take the presents down now . . . goodbye, Maestro. Are you looking forward to dinner? We'll see you later.'

'Yes, yes,' he said. 'I must rest now. Tonight will be a wonderful meal, true?'

'Oh, yes,' said Marianne. 'It's always lovely on Christmas Eve. Bye-bye.'

The old man waved at them as they left the room, carrying the presents in a pillowcase Marianne had brought up specially.

'Right,' she said, as she knelt to put the parcels on the growing pile in the Front Hall. 'We'll have to pretend to be surprised and delighted by these boxes of soap, or whatever they are.'

'Very posh soap, it looked,' Carlo said. 'Did Carrie get it in the village shop?'

'As if! No, Mail Order Queen of the Universe, that's Carrie. The village shop has a sign outside it that says: *Guaranteed, nothing in here you'll want to buy.*'

Carlo laughed. He was considering whether he could possibly put his hand out to touch Marianne's when she stood up.

'What,' he mumbled. 'I mean, what are you going to do now?'

'I'm going to make a phone call, but I'll see you later. Are you coming to the Midnight Service?'

'I will if I can sit next to you.'

'Right,' she said. 'Sure.'

She hurried away, up the stairs. Carlo wondered if she was going to phone *him* . . . the bloke Laurie had mentioned. Never mind, he thought, I'm going to sit next to her in church. She said I could. Yesss!

He made his way to the Library to see if Laurie was there. I'll ask him, he thought, who the young Maestro reminds him of. There was an image of someone, just on the edge of his mind, but as Carlo tried to catch hold of it and see who it was, it slipped infuriatingly away from him.

4.15 p.m. The Kitchen

There was a telephone extension in almost every room, and Marianne had thought carefully about which one was the most private. This one, in the kitchen, was perfect. The time was exactly right. Soon, Nana would be here dealing with the final touches to supper, but now she was faffing around with Olivia upstairs. As far as she could see, it was safe.

She picked up the receiver and put it down again. She had never, never done this before. She'd never had to. Boys always telephoned her, and if she didn't feel like it, she wouldn't even speak to them. Tell them I'm out, she used to say to Laurie, and dutifully he did. But Andy . . . he had to *know* that she'd try . . . that the roads were closed, but she'd try, and that if she couldn't make it to La Bodega, maybe they could spend New Year's Eve together. Would she have the nerve to suggest that? Right, Marianne, she said to herself. Nothing to it. Dial the number. Ask for Andy. Explain.

She took a deep breath and put the receiver to her ear. Silence. She put the handset down and picked it up again. Silence. She jiggled the jiggly bits . . . what were those called? . . . and nothing. Absolutely nothing. She traced the wire to the wall. There it was. No one had cut it.

'I do not believe it,' she whispered. 'The phone isn't working!'

Then she shouted it out: 'THE BLOODY PHONE ISN'T WORKING!'

Pamina, who had been asleep on some blankets beside the stove, woke up and looked at her.

'Sorry, Pamina, darling,' Marianne said. 'It's not your fault. It's the snow. I hate it.'

Pamina stood up and stretched. Then she padded over to the kitchen door and looked pleadingly at Marianne.

'Do you need to go out, kitty? Into all that horrible white wet stuff?'

She opened the door and Pamina left with her tail in the air. For a long time, she'd been using her cat flap to come back into the house, but still preferred a kind human to help her on the way out. Marianne watched her go, then shut the back door and left the kitchen and went to find someone she could take her bad temper out on. Maybe Laurie had finished his wrapping. She stamped as loudly as she could all the way upstairs. What was she supposed to do about Andy now?

11.00 p.m. The Front Hall

This, Carlo thought, pulling on a pair of Frederick's old wellingtons, is what setting out on an expedition must be like. For the last quarter of an hour, Irene had stood in the Front Hall ordering everyone about, distributing gloves, scarves and extra layers of clothing of one kind and another to anyone she thought might be underdressed.

'Derek,' she said. 'Here's a fur hat . . . from Russia. Much warmer than yours . . . take it, take it.'

Derek took it and put it on, even though it made him look slightly ridiculous.

We are, thought Carlo, like the Michelin family out on a spree. Marianne was unrecognizable in a puffy anorak and a football scarf and boots that looked as though they'd been made from yaks' feet. The only person who seemed halfway normal was Irene herself in a floor-length, fur-lined cape of midnight-blue velvet, which was once part of her costume in a more than ordinarily lavish production of *Don Giovanni*. ('Don't all look at me like that, darlings . . . you know I wouldn't wear *real* fur . . . false, false, false, but blissfully warm and you know how freezing churches always are . . .') She pulled up the hood and held it close under her chin.

'Ready?' she said at last, and everyone agreed that yes, whatever they did, they couldn't possibly be any more bundled up. Irene opened the front door and they all set out into the darkness and the cold. Down through the garden, across the lawn at the bottom of the terrace, round beside the Lake they went, making deep footprints in the white, and keeping their heads tucked down into their chests, struggling to keep noses and cheeks warm.

11.40 p.m. The Kitchen
'How long,' the Maestro asked, 'before the end of Act Three?'

He was sitting on the old sofa. That, Nana felt, was what was confusing him. It used to be the sofa in Irene's dressing room, backstage, long before it was put in the Library and then in here, when it became too tatty for the public rooms.

'You're in the kitchen, Maestro,' Nana said. 'It's Christmas Eve and the others are at the church. Irene is singing a carol. She always sings a carol every year. Don't you remember?'

'Of course, of course.' The Maestro looked put out for a

moment, and then his eye fell on the carrycot, which Nana had placed near the table.

'My baby?' he said. 'We are looking after her? What a beautiful baby!'

'You haven't got a baby, Maestro. Don't you remember? This isn't your baby.'

The Maestro shook his head, puzzled. Nana sighed. Was there any point at all in explaining about Olivia? How her mother had run away, how she and her father were staying in the Golden House? No, she decided. It's too complicated for him. Why should I bother? What difference does it make to anything if he thinks it's his own baby we're babysitting for? Why shouldn't he imagine he's a father? You could wear yourself out trying to keep the Maestro in the real world.

It's true, what they say, she thought. There really is always someone worse off than yourself. Nana had been feeling worried and sick, but there you are. The pain had mostly held off (keep your fingers crossed, you silly old woman!) and at least she still had all her marbles.

'Pamina! Pamina, where are you? You haven't eaten your food. Pamina!' She turned to the Maestro. 'Have you seen the cat?' Nana had to call her 'the cat'. For the Maestro, Pamina was the princess from *The Magic Flute*.

'No,' said the Maestro. 'I haven't seen her for a long time.'

'I expect she's upstairs on one of the beds,' said Nana. 'She'll appear when they come back from church.'

11.45 p.m. All Saints Church

Carlo, Laurie and Marianne were in a bunch together at the back of the crocodile.

'Is that a *lantern*?' Carlo asked. 'Is Irene carrying an actual lantern?'

'Naturally,' said Marianne. 'Props and costumes have to be exactly right.'

'It's Rule Number Two', Laurie added, 'of the Life as Theatre Philosophy.'

'What's Rule Number One?' Carlo smiled.

'Do you need to ask?' Laurie put on a stage voice. 'The Show Must Go On. That's it. Always. About everything. Haven't you noticed? Look at us now. Any sensible person wouldn't go out on a night like this. Ellie's miserable, so is Susanna, and my mum and dad are hardly civil to one another, Lord knows why, but here we are trudging... that's the only word for it... off to church looking like a Christmas card. I cannot for the life of me think why.'

'Because,' Marianne said, 'we always have. This is the night, the one night of the year when The Voice comes out of mothballs and everyone over forty-five wipes a nostalgic tear from their eye. Irene would have to be in her coffin before she missed it.'

Carlo wondered what would happen at church. It was years and years since he'd been. Would he know what to do and when? Would Marianne remember that she'd promised to sit next to him, or should he remind her? Or would that be the height of uncool? I'll stick very close to her, he thought. I won't let anyone else slip in between us. He noticed that Laurie was sticking very close to *him*. Well, he can sit on my other side, I suppose. Carlo hoped, fervently, that Letta and Derek wouldn't suddenly want to be near their daughter.

And it came to pass in those days, that there went out a decree from Caesar Augustus, that all the world should be taxed.

Derek tried to feel as he usually felt in an old church: soothed by the ancient stone, interested in the memorial carvings and the stained glass, and comforted by the voice of a child reading the familiar words. He couldn't. Anger at Letta, and a sort of hopeless sorrow, was taking up most of his head.

The children need to know, he thought, and tried to remember what he'd read in a thousand Sunday newspapers about divorce. Was it better to do it when the children were young? Or when they were teenagers? Look at poor old Ellie. She wasn't exactly on top form but, of course, her father was in America. He, Derek, had no intention of losing touch with Marianne and Laurie. Something Ellie's father used to say came back to him: whichever way you slice it, he used to say, it's still baloney. He'd spoken like an American long before he went off to the United States.

And there were in the same country shepherds abiding in the field, keeping watch over their flocks by night.

What would she do if the phone remained out of order? Letta looked at her daughter and wondered how long she could keep up the pretence. Marianne knew she was lying yesterday. Why hasn't she said anything? Letta wondered.

Is she waiting to see what I'll do? Has Derek said something to the children without telling me? It never occurred to her that Marianne was busy with concerns of her own. Surely, she said to herself, surely anyone trying to phone would realize that the line was down . . .

And this shall be a sign unto you; Ye shall find the babe wrapped in swaddling clothes, lying in a manger.

Ellie wondered whether Olivia had swaddling clothes. What were they? Nana would know. Edmund hadn't had to go and be taxed, and his little baby didn't have a manger to sleep in, but still, they weren't in their own home. Poor old Mary and Joseph! Ellie wondered about nappies and night feeds and how they used to look after babies in the olden days, before sterilized bottles and disposables had been invented. The Bible didn't bother with stuff like that. She hadn't even dared to look at the crib on the way in, in case it made her burst into tears all over again. She'd never thought about it before, but Christmas was about a baby being born, so it was hard to forget what Susanna had told her.

Think about something else, Ellie, she told herself. Think about nice things. The best thing, talking to Dad on the phone tomorrow, wouldn't be happening. The snow had broken the lines. Would praying do any good? Ellie doubted it but, just in case, she closed her eyes and made a sort of holy-sounding wish.

Glory to God in the Highest, and on earth peace, good will toward men.

*

Laurie would never have admitted it, but it got to him. The whole thing: dark corners, candlelight, his favourite angel up there near the top of a column with carved wooden wings outspread, the picture of the Good Samaritan in stained glass that you couldn't see at night, but which, in daylight, was a mass of blisteringly bright colours, the crib in the entrance (courtesy of a local school) with its chubby, plastic Baby Jesus and its black-and-white cows, and, more than anything, the music. He couldn't help it. The sound the organ made reduced him to tears, and he found it hard to sing the carols he loved because of the lump in his throat. You're a sucker, he told himself. A sucker for Theatre, like Irene, like almost everyone.

He'd been feeling dissatisfied, out of sorts. Why weren't he and Carlo spending all their time together? He'd been dreaming about that since Bonfire Night. The rituals of the service distracted him. Tomorrow, he decided, he would do it – tell Carlo how he felt. Sometime tomorrow he would find a time, and speak to him.

Now, when Jesus was born in Bethlehem of Judaea in the days of Herod the king, behold, there came wise men from the east to Jerusalem.

Susanna looked at her daughter. It was obvious that she'd been crying, but at least she was here. She was wearing make-up, which made her appear younger and more vulnerable than usual. Marianne had spoken to her. Ellie always listened to Marianne.

Susanna smiled when she remembered Ellie's first Midnight Service. Nana had agreed to take her back to the

Golden House the minute she showed signs of fretting . . . she had just turned five. They tiptoed up the aisle during the third lesson and, when they'd almost reached the door, Ellie had turned to the altar and called out in a ringing voice, that Irene always said was inherited from her, 'Night, night, Baby Jesus . . . I'm going home now!'

Everyone laughed, and the vicar called back to her: 'Bless you, Ellie dear.'

Tears came to Susanna's eyes. Yes, she thought, yes. Bless you, my darling child.

And when they were come into the house, they saw the young child with Mary his mother, and fell down and worshipped him.

Carrie had gone over and over what Edmund had said to her that morning outside the gazebo. His kiss had made her feel as though a sort of electric current had passed through her body. It was, she supposed you could say, shocking. Carrie was in the habit of looking for accurate ways of expressing things, and this described exactly what had happened to her.

All day she had walked around dazed, cuddling Olivia, feeding her, and imagining things she had trained herself never to imagine – herself and Edmund as man and wife. He had said (Had he said? Or had she invented it? Misremembered?) something about his feelings for her. Perhaps one day, after he and Serena had legalized the separation . . . well, he hadn't mentioned divorce, but that was surely what he meant. Wasn't it? Don't run ahead of yourself, Carrie, she thought. You've done it before and suffered for it. Enjoy the moment. She looked sideways at Edmund, standing so close to her that she imagined she could feel his warmth. She felt like shouting out: I love him! Listen to me, everyone. I love him!

And when they had opened their treasures, they presented unto him gifts; gold and frankincense and myrrh.

Marianne had decided that, as there was nothing to be done about Andy for the time being, she might as well enjoy herself. From time to time, she looked sideways at Carlo and it didn't matter what was happening in the order of service, he was always gazing at her. She'd whispered to him at one point. Why, she'd asked him, are you always looking at me? He'd answered, also in a whisper: because you're beautiful. Quick as a flash! Stacey would never believe her. Boys only said stuff like that in the kind of soppy romantic books she wouldn't be seen dead reading. She hadn't known what to do, so she carried on singing 'Hark the herald angels sing', with her heart beating rather fast.

And then, when they were kneeling for prayers, just at the bit when the vicar was asking them to pray for the Royal Family, it happened. Her left hand was hanging down and so was Carlo's right hand, and then he was touching her. His fingers twined themselves around hers. Could anyone else see? Could Laurie? Carlo was holding her hand. He held it until the end of the prayer, and stroked the inside of his palm with one of his fingers. She felt herself blushing, and smiled at him, sideways, without turning her head. Oh, wow! she thought. Wait till I tell Stacey! Marianne was finding it more and more difficult to focus on what was going on all round her. It was as though the whole of her was concentrated in her left-hand side, which was practically touching him and felt as if it was glowing . . . oh wow and double wow!

The service was almost over. The congregation (Irene couldn't help thinking of it as 'the audience') wasn't as big as it usually was, but that was because of the snow. Still, enough people had come to convince her that she was still capable of it: drawing the crowds. She made her way to the steps below the altar and arranged the heavy folds of the cloak around herself. The organist nodded his head and began to play the introduction. Irene looked up at the vaulted roof and began to sing:

> *'In the bleak midwinter,*
> *frosty wind made moan.*
> *Earth stood hard as iron,*
> *water like a stone.*
> *Snow had fallen, snow on snow,*
> *snow on snow.*
> *In the bleak midwinter*
> *long ago.'*

She felt the music come from her, rise up, and circle in the air like a golden bird. She felt she could sing forever, as though there were nothing else at all in her whole body but this wonderful, reverberating sound, which soared and flew and dipped, and fell at last into a perfect silence. No one clapped in church, of course, but Irene had been a performer for long enough to know that she had stunned them; stunned them all. She bowed from the waist, and when she stood up straight again, her eyes were full of unshed tears.

While Irene sang, Carlo found himself unable to think of anything but the music she was making. Marianne, Laurie, the Golden House, Christmas, his mother, his school, even *himself* . . . they all vanished and his whole being was filled with the most glorious noise he had ever heard. When the last note and the last words . . . *gi-i-ive my heart* . . . died away, it was like waking up from the most beautiful dream. Why had no one told him? Was this what opera was like as well? Were there perhaps old records of that voice? I'll ask Marianne, he thought. As soon as her name came into his mind, he became aware, once again, of her presence beside him, but the carol Irene had sung was still with him. It'll always be with me, he thought. A perfect memory. Carlo wished that you could take photographs of sound without using a recording studio.

After the service, the procession made its way back to the Golden House, once again wrapped up against the cold.

'What happens now?' Carlo asked. 'Does everyone go to sleep?'

'Oh, no,' said Laurie, struggling to keep up with his sister and Carlo . . . why had they taken it into their heads to *stride*? 'We have to have warm drinks and Nana's special Christmas Eve flan.'

Marianne sighed. 'More food. It's all Nana ever thinks about. If you looked into her head, what you'd see would be hundreds and hundreds of hand-written menus and recipes. It's disgusting.'

'My sister,' Laurie explained, 'is teetering on the verge of anorexia.'

Marianne bent down and made a snowball and began to stuff it down the front of Laurie's coat.

'Help!' he cried. 'Carlo, help me! Throw something at her!'

Carlo obliged with a snowball, which hit Marianne over the head, and soon all three were giggling and shrieking so much, as they scooped white handfuls and lobbed them at one another, that Irene called out: 'Stop, children! Stop at once. You'll wake the entire neighbourhood.'

No more snowballs were thrown, but the muffled laughter continued.

Laurie said, under his breath: 'Neighbourhood . . . don'cha just love it? Anyone would think she was living in the Bronx. Never mind. Irene has spoken. Forward to warm drinks and Christmas flan.'

Carlo took Marianne's hand and pulled her back as the others went into the house.

'Wait!' he whispered. 'Please wait.'

'You're mad . . . they're all just there, inside the door.'

'I don't care,' Carlo said. 'Please.' He put both hands on her shoulders.

'Marianne. Please . . .' He kissed her briefly on the lips, and felt her trembling.

They stepped into the hall together.

CHRISTMAS DAY

Christmas Meal

Grapefruit cocktail

Brazil-nut-and-savoury-stuffing loaf
Roast potatoes, roast parsnips,
Brussels sprouts with chestnuts
Fresh-herb gravy

Christmas pudding
Brandy butter
*

Coffee

1.00 a.m. The Garden

Pamina's green eyes were nearly closing with the effort of finding the right place. She didn't know who this person was. It was no one she recognized. She sniffed all round the Lady's feet, and they seemed to be as cold as the ground on which she stood. Here was something: a stiff garment of some kind, spread out on the ground. Should she tread herself a nest? Did she have enough strength in her feet? No, she thought. It's like a curtain, and I will lie down behind it and rest.

She squeezed herself between the curtain and the icy bulk

of the Lady's skirt, and curled up on the snow with the heavy folds of the Queen of the Night's silver cloak hiding her silver fur. She closed her eyes. The cold moved from her paws and spread itself through her body. It was making her strangely drowsy. The time for sleeping had come.

The wind blew in from the west, piling any loose snow into deep drifts. All through the night, telephone engineers had been working on the lines, but still the people who were trying to reach the Golden House were disappointed.

6.30 a.m. The Brown Room

'Laurie? Are you awake?' Carlo whispered.

'I've been awake for ages, but what's the matter with you?'

'I always wake up early on Christmas Day. When I was little', Carlo said, 'I used to have a stocking full of Dinky cars and sweets.'

'But you know,' Laurie said, 'that presents come after breakfast. First, Presents. Then Preparation, then Party. Irene's Iron Law for a day that's meant to be amazingly spontaneous. I told you.'

'Yeah, but I'm excited. I can't help it.'

'Me too,' said Laurie. Silence grew in the space between their beds. Was this, Laurie wondered, a good time to speak? What should he say? How could he explain? And what would Carlo do? He couldn't run away, because the roads were blocked. He couldn't even phone his mum to complain . . . not that he'd do anything like that. Of course not. Carlo wasn't homophobic . . . they'd had discussions, debates in school . . . oh, very general. Nothing personal, all done in the context of class discussion, but Carlo didn't seem to have any hang-ups. But maybe if it was *him* he'd feel altogether different.

Laurie took a deep breath. I'm going to say it, he thought. I've got to, whatever happens, even if it's what Marianne calls a Worst Case Scenario.

He had already opened his mouth to speak, when Carlo said: 'Laurie? Can I tell you something?'

Oh, God, Laurie thought. Really? Could it be? Could *Carlo* possibly be? He swallowed and began to blush all over in anticipation. Rather breathlessly, he said: 'Sure . . . anything. You know that.'

'OK.' Carlo sat up in bed and hugged his knees through the duvet. 'Promise you won't be angry.'

I don't believe it, Laurie thought. I just don't believe this. He's going to save me the trouble. He sat up as well, to underline the importance of the moment. It would never do to hear something like this lying down.

'I'd never, ever be angry with you,' he said.

'No matter what?'

'No matter what.'

'OK,' Carlo said again, and turned to face Laurie. 'It's Marianne.'

For a moment, Laurie couldn't take it in. What on earth had Marianne to do with any of this?

'What about her?' Laurie said.

'I kissed her last night.'

'When?'

'Just before we came in, after church. Everyone was in the Hall. I thought for sure someone would come out and see us.'

Laurie felt as though every word he uttered was being squeezed up out of his throat. He said: 'That was all a bit sudden, wasn't it?'

'Not really. I've wanted to kiss her since I very first laid eyes on her. When we were up in the attic together, something . . . I don't know what exactly . . . sort of passed between us . . . like sort of electricity. Then, in church, I stroked her hand and she didn't seem to mind. So I just went for it. I didn't dare tell you. I don't know why. I should have known you wouldn't mind. You don't, do you?'

Laurie gulped.

'Mind? Me? Perish the thought!'

He lay back against his pillows and stared at the ceiling. There was a bitter taste in his mouth. So much for Christmas Cheer, he thought. At least he hadn't said anything to Carlo. What a *fool* he would have felt, saying it . . . I love you. What would Carlo have thought of him? Would he have turned on him? Called him a poofter, or worse? At least he'd been spared *that* particular humiliation. But how was he going to get through the rest of the day, not to mention the rest of his life? The first and most immediate problem was how to get through the next few minutes without bursting into tears.

9.00 a.m. The Dining Room

'Where's Pamina?' Ellie asked. 'I haven't seen her for ages.'

'I saw her yesterday,' Marianne said. She was busy dividing the contents of Nana's pretty little Christmas basket into things she could eat (satsumas and raisins) and others she was intending to give to Laurie, or Ellie, or whoever would take them . . . glacéd chestnuts, for heaven's sake! Who needed such things?

'Her food is still there,' Nana said. 'She hasn't eaten anything since yesterday.'

'She's lost!' said Ellie. 'I know she is . . . we must go and find her. Who's going to come with me and find her?'

'Ellie dear,' said Irene, 'Pamina is hiding away somewhere, I'm quite sure. We haven't got time now for a full-scale search of the house. She's fond of cupboards, you know, and she often lies under the duvets as well. Don't worry about her. She's a very old cat and a very wise cat.'

Laurie could see that Irene's words hadn't exactly cheered Ellie up. She frowned, and bit her lip.

'I'll come, Ellie,' he whispered, when the searchlight of Irene's attention had moved on to someone else. 'I'll help you look after we've done the presents. There's always time while they get stuff ready for the meal.'

'But I'm supposed to be helping . . .'

'No one will notice. It'll be chaos in the kitchen. My mum and your mum and Carrie . . . they'll all be flapping about trying to help Nana and getting in the way. I'm sure we'll find her. Don't let it spoil the presents.'

'OK,' said Ellie. 'I'll try.'

She looked unconvinced. It occurred to Laurie that maybe *that* was when you stopped being a kid: when the idea of unwrapping lots of presents wasn't enough to stop you hurting inside. He looked around the table. How many of the others would describe themselves as happy? Carrie certainly was. There she sat at the top of the table with Olivia in her arms, and she'd even dressed in pale blue: the medieval Madonna-and-child look. Full marks to the baby, as well. She could have been especially designed in a Theatrical Properties factory to sit and gurgle placidly in someone's arms looking bonny and hardly ever crying . . . just the thing for bringing out everyone's parental instincts.

Susanna still looked haunted, and the Maestro appeared to be more bewildered than usual. Carlo and Marianne he couldn't bear even to think about. They were glowing, that was the only word for it. I must ask Marianne, he thought. Ask her what she feels. Or maybe I don't want to know. I feel like a giant squeezed lemon . . . all dry and yellow and SOUR.

10.00 a.m. The Chinese Lounge

Irene's reaction to the Christmas Tree was, in Laurie's opinion, somewhat extreme. Dressed in what he thought of as her Yuletide Gorgeousness of bronze-coloured floor-length velvet (to match the brocade slip covers on the sofa), she led the way into the Chinese Lounge, then sort of staggered back a pace or two with her hand over her mouth in a gesture that Laurie felt sure came from some moment of revelation in one or another opera. Then she stood still for a very long time, just staring, and everyone else stood around her with their mouths open.

'I have never,' she said at last, 'in a long, long lifetime ever seen anything like that, Marianne darling. You are to be congratulated.' She wiped a tear from her eye.

'OTT, as usual,' Laurie whispered to Ellie, 'our dear granny.'

'But it does look . . .' Ellie gazed at the tree with round eyes.

Laurie tried to be objective; to put entirely out of his

head any resentment he was feeling towards his sister. She had tied thousands and thousands of ribbons from the branches: some done up in bows, some just trailing down. Most of them were pink or blue or white, but there were many red ribbons and also a scattering of gold and silver ones. The contrast with the dark-green pine needles was startling and (Laurie had to admit it) most beautiful.

It was Carrie who put everyone's thoughts into words. 'It's like something from a dream,' she announced in uncharacteristically firm tones.

Irene had meanwhile had time to examine everything more closely by now and she exclaimed: 'Oh, there's the ribbon from the first night of *La Traviata*! And look, that's the one you gave me, Frederick, when we did *Marriage of Figaro*. I can't believe it, Marianne. It's as though you've tied every one of my memories from these branches! You are so *clever*, darling!'

After that, she arranged everyone on sofas and chairs for the Presents. Laurie sat next to Ellie, thinking how well he was managing to hold himself together when his heart was broken and his life lay in ruins, rather like that clown chap who went on smiling through the tears. He even managed to summon up enthusiasm for the gifts. According to tradition, these were given out according to age, beginning with Irene and Frederick and Nana, and working downwards.

'Do other families do this?' Ellie asked. 'Buy everyone the same present, I mean? I know I've done it, but that's because we have to make ours.'

'I think it's a good idea,' said Laurie. 'Especially when the gift is jewellery.'

Irene had divided the family into male and female: gold

bracelets for the women and gold cufflinks for the men. 'Only', he added, 'I'll have to buy a new shirt now with cuffs to put these links in.'

Nana had been knitting scarves and mittens, and Susanna had bought wonderful notebooks for everyone, with marbled covers and gold-edged pages.

'Brilliant!' Laurie kissed his aunt. 'At last! A book worthy of my deathless prose.'

Frederick had opted for toiletries, and Letta and Derek had taken the easy way out and given everyone music and book tokens.

'Unimaginative,' Laurie muttered to Ellie, 'but perhaps the very best presents of all in the end.'

Carrie gave out her parcels with her head bowed. You could always tell which were hers, even under the tree. They were the most tastefully wrapped of all, this year in delicate mauve tissue paper and silver string.

'*The White Room*,' Irene's voice rang out, 'by someone called C. G. I had no idea people still used initials . . . how very nineteenth-century!' She opened the book. 'My dear, it's *poetry*!'

'What a pretty cover!' Letta exclaimed. 'Thank you so much, Carrie.'

Derek looked carefully at the poems.

'How interesting these look,' he said. 'Not like any poems I've seen before. Do you know anything at all about the author? Initials are so enigmatic.'

'I like books,' said Letta, 'with pictures of the author on the cover. I'm always so nosy about what the person looks like . . . aren't you?'

'I can tell you about the author,' said Carrie. 'It's me. I wrote the poems.'

Shrieking and squeaking broke out all over the Chinese Lounge. Carrie spent the next few minutes being interrogated: when had she written them and why, and how did she know where to send them, and was she being paid, and would she be famous ... until at last Irene restored order by saying: 'It's too, too marvellous, Carrie, but we must move on or we'll be here all day. Let's move on to the children's presents.'

Derek said: 'There was a time when those words would have struck terror into the stoutest heart ... nothing but recycled egg-boxes and macaroni art!'

'I wouldn't count on anything much more ambitious than that from me, Dad,' Laurie said, as he handed out his chocolate-dipped orange peel. To his great relief, everyone expressed themselves delighted with it, and also with Marianne's needlepoint bookmarks. *Needlepoint? Marianne?* Laurie asked himself as he unwrapped his. How very unexpected! People kept surprising you. Ellie's painted plaster birds were much admired, but if there had been a Gold Medal for gifts, it would certainly have gone to Carlo. Everyone loved his stained-glass ornaments.

'You're supposed,' he said, 'to hang them at a window, then the light shines through them.'

Irene held up her apple, and said: 'Darling, how beautiful! How clever of you. I shall treasure it forever.'

Laurie's present was not like the others. It was a star made from opalescent glass that was nearly pink. He looked at it for a long time without saying anything.

'It's for you to wish on,' Carlo said gently, and Laurie

111

answered: 'I know. It's easily the best present I've ever had. Thank you.'

He thought: but I can never have what I wish for, not even with the help of my pearly star.

Marianne's gift from Carlo was a red rose, and she blushed when she saw it.

'How romantic, sweetheart!' Letta exclaimed, and her daughter looked for a moment as though she was about to get up from her chair and strangle her mother with a bit of glittery string.

'Pamina likes all the unwrapping,' Ellie said. 'Where is she? I want to go and look for her.'

'Very well, dear,' said Irene. 'You go and search about upstairs. I don't think we'll be eating before about three o'clock, will we, Nana?'

Nana shook her head silently.

'Is anything wrong, Nana?' said Susanna.

'No, no, dear,' said Nana. 'It's nothing. Just a little . . . headache. I must go and take an aspirin.'

'You're looking very pale,' said Letta. 'We'll all come and help in the kitchen, won't we? Marianne? Laurie?'

'I'm going with Ellie,' Laurie said.

'I'll come,' said Carlo to Letta, and Laurie at least understood that what he was really saying was: wherever Marianne is going, I want to go too.

'Let's go, Ellie,' he said. 'Merry Christmas, everyone.'

The pale sun made every tree and bush in the white garden glitter, and deep in the heart of the ice, the melting had started. Hidden by the folds of the Snow Lady's cloak, Pamina's body was stiff, and her fur had frozen into prickles of grey.

112

1.00 p.m. The Kitchen

The Maestro nobbled Carlo just as he was on his way to the kitchen with Marianne. Still quite sure that he was talking to a musician called Alexei, Frederick began to discuss the finer points of his interpretation of Brahms's Violin Concerto. Part of Marianne was annoyed with Carlo for not putting the old man straight and coming with her, but she had to admire the way he was humouring the Maestro and acting the part to perfection. What it meant was that she was here with no one interesting to talk to, and listening to her mother bossing everyone around as usual.

'Nana, darling,' Letta said, 'you're not yourself at all . . . no, don't say a word. I can tell. We're going to do everything. Aren't we?' She beamed encouragingly at Susanna and Marianne.

'The potatoes won't be the same if I don't do them,' Nana said, rather weakly. 'There's nothing the matter with me.'

'Of course they won't be the same,' Susanna said, 'but we'll do the best we can. Sit on the sofa and give us your instructions.'

'It's all nonsense,' Letta whispered to Marianne. 'I've known Nana's potato secret since I was ten. There's nothing remotely mysterious about it. It's even in Delia Smith: par-boiled spuds and very hot fat.'

'Come on, Mum,' Marianne said. 'You know Nana likes her little kitchen rituals. It doesn't hurt anyone.'

'You're right, I know,' said Letta and sighed. 'But all this fussing over what you eat all the time . . . I find it exhausting.'

'Right,' said Marianne, pleased that for once she and her mother were in agreement about something.

Then Letta changed her tune, and said: 'But of course a properly healthy diet is amazingly important, especially when you're growing. I must say, I'm a little worried about you. You're fading away rather, aren't you?'

Marianne thought: grrr! How typical of Letta to be so inconsistent and turn fussy-mother-ish all of a sudden. Still, it was peace on earth and goodwill to all parents time, so she confined herself to saying sweetly: 'Not at all, Mum. My diet is perfectly adequate. Every nutrient under the sun, I promise. I just don't stuff my face that's all, which is a bit of a no-no in this house, isn't it?'

Letta had her mouth open ready to answer, but Marianne seized the opportunity and continued: 'Mum, I want to ask you something.'

'Does it have to be now?' Was Letta blushing, or was it the warmth from the oven?

'Yes, it does,' said Marianne. 'You're behaving very funnily. First of all, it *was* you coming back from the village early yesterday, wasn't it?'

'Yes,' said Letta. 'I went down to the phone box. I had to make a private phone call.'

Marianne ran water into a saucepan and put it on the hob to boil.

'Who to?' she said.

'Someone . . . it doesn't matter, truly.'

'It does to me.'

'But honestly, Marianne, this isn't the time or the place. There's . . . well, there's so much to explain. And . . . I want to talk to you and Laurie together, and I really don't think just before Christmas dinner is the proper occasion. Can you bear to wait?'

'It looks as though I'm going to have to.'

'Well find a quiet place tomorrow,' said Letta. 'I promise. There's never anything to do on Boxing Day, is there? I hate it. It's such an anti-climax and worse than ever this year because we can't even leave. Oh, I do wish all this ghastly snow would just melt overnight. Wouldn't that be marvellous?'

'Mmm,' said Marianne, not really listening any more, but wondering what it was Letta was going to tell them tomorrow. She felt a sense of foreboding: something like dread was beginning to creep up from the pit of her stomach, and spread out through her whole body. How much of this feast they were all busy putting together would she be able to eat?

1.30 p.m. The Garden

They had looked in every single corner of every single room, but Pamina was nowhere to be found. Ellie and Laurie, bundled up in coats and gloves, had walked down as far as the Lake and were now outside the gazebo.

'I thought', Laurie said, 'that cats hated the cold.'

'But there's nowhere else to go,' Ellie was sounding more and more tearful. 'Maybe she just went out for a minute and then got too cold to move. Perhaps she's in the gazebo.'

They opened the door and went in. Laurie said: 'I've only ever been in here in the summer. It's different, isn't it, with all the snow?' One of his favourite fantasies, in the weeks before Carlo had come to the Golden House, was of them sitting here together, away from the others, talking

115

about things he would never have spoken about to anybody else. There was no chance of that now. Marianne would probably bring Carlo here ... it was a good place to go, really, if you weren't keen on snogging under Irene's roof.

'She isn't here, Ellie,' he said at last. His cousin had sat down on one of the seats and was scratching patterns in the frost on the window.

'I hate it,' she said suddenly. 'I hate this whole Christmas and I wish it was over. It's horrible.' She sniffed.

'Ellie? Are you crying? Oh, Ellie.'

'I'm sorry. I can't help it, but everything is going wrong and now poor Pamina is missing. Where has she gone? She never goes anywhere. I can't bear it if she's out there somewhere in the snow. Now you probably think I'm a baby, crying over a cat.'

'Pamina's not just a cat ... what a suggestion!' said Laurie. He went to sit beside her, and put an arm around her shoulders. 'For two pins I'd bawl along with you. We could bawl in harmony.'

Ellie turned to look at him.

'Oh, no, Laurie ... not you ... you're always so cheerful. You make me laugh. What is it?'

'The way I feel, you're going to have to advertise for a new jester, milady!'

Ellie bit her lip.

'Is it Carlo? Has he ... I mean does he ... I'm sorry, I don't know how to say this, but are you jealous?'

Laurie laughed. 'I am, as a matter of fact. How on earth did you guess? I thought I was doing a good job of being inscrutable.'

'You are, but Marianne ...'

116

'What has she told you? Go on, you can tell me.'

'I can't.'

'Why not?'

'It's . . . well, it's not something you can say straight out like that.'

Laurie smiled. 'Then I bet I know what it is. And you're right, it is *embarrassing*, though I really don't have any idea why it should be.' He took a deep breath. 'Right, Ellie dear, you're in luck. I'm going to do it. I'm going to tell you. They call it 'coming out' but I can't bear that expression. Are you ready for this? OK. I think I'm gay. No, correction, I *am* gay. Now for heaven's sake say something.'

'I don't know what to say,' Ellie grinned. 'Do you feel better, now you've said it?'

'I do, actually, only you're not the real test. What will my dad say? Will he throw a fit? Do I care if he does?'

'Do you?'

'No, not really.' Laurie stood up. 'I feel . . . I feel relieved. I used to think . . . part of me still thinks, I suppose, that something awful would happen to me if I was . . . well, a bit different from everybody else.'

'But you're *not* different. Or rather, you *are*, but not because of being gay. You're different because you're you.'

'I know. You're right, of course. I should feel better and I do in a way. But I'm no less jealous even though I feel more *honest* about it. I was meant to be cheering *you* up. What's wrong?'

'Did you know,' Ellie said, 'that my mother has just had an abortion?'

Laurie sat down again.

'No, I didn't. Oh, God, Ellie, how awful for her!'

Ellie frowned. 'You see, you immediately think of her!'

'Who am I supposed to think of?'

'The baby! Me!'

'It wasn't a baby, Ellie. It hadn't grown into one. Not yet. You mustn't think of it like that.'

'But I could have had a sister. Or a brother.'

Laurie sighed. 'Marianne is not in my good books at the moment, as you can imagine, but I wouldn't be without her. Still, for all practical purposes, and not just to make you feel happier, let me assure you that I am quite ready to be your devoted brother. You may call on for anything. You are my very favourite non-sibling sister.'

Ellie flung her arms round Laurie and hugged him.

'Oh, I do love you, Laurie! And I feel a bit better. If only we could find Pamina safe and sound, I'd promise not to moan about anything ever again.'

'Of course you'll moan,' said Laurie. 'But how does a Christmas meal in the bosom of your family sound? I call that an offer you can't refuse.'

3.30 p.m. The Dining Room

Even Nana had to admit that the potatoes were well up to standard: golden and crispy on the outside, with many satisfyingly dark-brown burnt patches, and soft and white in the middle. They had now all but vanished. A few sprouts and chestnut pieces lay in the buttery bowls that had been overflowing until a few minutes ago. Nana's legendary Brazil-nut loaf with its succulent layer of fresh-herb stuffing had been pronounced the best ever. Wine (white for everyone except Letta and Carrie, who preferred red, and Marianne who never drank anything at the dinner table but juice or still mineral water) had sparkled and fizzed in the best crystal glasses, and everyone was feeling pleasantly full.

'We've got pudding to contend with now,' Laurie said to Carlo, who was sitting to his left. 'Not to mention brandy butter.'

'This is the best Christmas meal I've ever had,' Carlo said. Laurie could see that he was trying to catch Marianne's eye across the table, but she was talking to Susanna and taking not a blind bit of notice. He gave up and turned to Laurie again.

'Did you find Pamina?'

Laurie shook his head. 'I'm sure she's still in the house somewhere. I can't see her staying out in the snow.' He took a gulp of wine.

'I expect she'll turn up,' said Carlo, but his attention was on the Maestro, sitting quietly and staring into space, near the top of the table. Who was it that the old man resembled? He felt that if he concentrated hard enough, it would come to him. It was there, on the very edges of his mind, and if only he sent his thoughts in the right direction, the answer would be there. Maybe if he *stopped* thinking, it would just pop into his head.

'It's been a wonderful Christmas,' Edmund smiled at Carrie, 'thanks to you and all your family. I certainly couldn't have managed without you. You've been . . . well, more than kind to us. Look at Olivia. She is so peaceful and quiet here.'

'I'm sure she's always like that,' said Carrie, blushing.

'No, no,' said Edmund. 'I've known her cry for hours. You are a very soothing presence. To me, as much as to her. But I wanted to say something about your poems.'

119

Carrie bent her head and began to crush a last morsel of potato with her fork.

'They are very accomplished, you know. Very strange and beautiful.'

'Thank you,' said Carrie. 'I wrote them entirely for myself. I really . . .' She stopped abruptly. How could she explain without seeming rude that her poems were the one thing about her which was *certain?* The one thing about which she felt no anxiety whatsoever? The one piece of her life where she could honestly say she didn't give a damn about the opinions of other people? She had rehearsed in her mind what the reaction of her mother and sisters would be. She had steeled herself for ridicule, or amazement, or praise or jealousy, but the one thing she hadn't predicted was the almost universal lack of interest in the poems themselves.

She gazed round the table at her family. Laurie would read them carefully. So would Derek. Derek would mark them out of ten and tell her of any shortcomings in order to help her to improve. None of the others would bother. Her sisters would try, then put the book aside saying wasn't Carrie clever but it really wasn't their sort of thing. Irene's reaction would depend on whether or not a fuss was made of the book. If it won a prize, say, then she would sing its praises to everyone she met. Otherwise, she'd forget about it.

Carrie smiled and took another sip of wine. Never mind, she thought. The poems are there. The book exists. A child is the child of two people, but these words come from me and no one else. These words are mine.

BOXING DAY

Menus for the Day

LUNCH
Various salads/leftovers/tomato-and-basil quiche

DINNER
Spaghetti arrabiata
Winter salad

Lemon cake
Coffee and petits fours

A thaw had begun. The Snow Lady's head was beginning to slump forward. Engineers were at work on the telephone lines, and soon the Golden House would be reconnected to the outside world.

5.00 a.m. Irene's Room

Irene had never been a good sleeper and, as she grew older, her nights became shorter and shorter. A kind of nervousness about what the day ahead would bring made her restless. She was worried about Pamina. Then there was the baby. Having someone crying in the early morning wasn't exactly designed to promote peaceful sleep. And she had always hated Boxing Day. If Christmas was a performance, then the day that followed it was like the dead time between the end of one show and the beginning of rehearsals for the next.

There was clearing up to be done. Irene didn't hold with letting things hang on till Twelfth Night. To her mind, decorations became tawdry the minute the clock struck midnight on Christmas Day . . . like Cinderella, the tree seen in the light of day would probably look as if it were dressed in rags. It would have to be dismantled as soon as possible. Maybe even tomorrow. Marianne would be upset if she took it down today.

Irene sighed. She would go and hunt for Pamina in those places that the others knew nothing about. No one understood this house as well as she did. She put on her robe and left the room. She walked silently through the corridors, looking in the empty rooms, behind the curtains, and in the half-open cupboards. As she passed Carrie's room, she thought of the poems. What a strange person Carrie was . . . had always been. Of course she hadn't had more than a glance at the book, but it seemed to her to reflect a certain . . . eccentricity.

Irene smiled to herself as she often did when she considered other people's stupidity. Could they really not see what was in front of their eyes? To her the resemblance between Carrie and Frederick was striking. Why had no one guessed that she was his daughter? Nana knew, Irene was convinced of it. She had been Irene's only confidant while the affair was at its height, but she had never mentioned it and perhaps had almost forgotten it ever happened. To tell the truth, Irene herself found it hard to remember how she had felt all those years ago. Nowadays, the Maestro was a poor old man and she took care of him. Summoning up those passionate embraces of thirty years ago was pointless. Thank God, *he* wasn't likely to say anything, and if something should slip out by accident, well, he was a touch ga-ga, wasn't he? Always talking nonsense. Hardly anyone listened to what he said these days.

One of the advantages of their new life would be that Frederick would be properly looked after. Tonight, Irene decided. I shall tell them tonight. It won't be easy. She smiled when she thought of the performance she would have to give, and her mind turned to what to wear for such an occasion. Black silk, she thought. With pearls. She continued along the corridors. Where was Pamina?

10.00 a.m. The Brown Room

Laurie opened the notebook Susanna had given him and wondered whether it was OK to start writing in such a grand-looking book when what you wanted to do, basically, was MOAN. He decided against it, and put it away with a sigh. Another day. If he was going to last till he was seventy, that was another nearly twenty thousand to go before he popped his clogs. How exhausting! How would he manage to fill them? He picked up Carrie's slim volume, and opened it at random.

> *some fires, lit in grey shadow*
> *burn invisible; put out shoots*
> *sucking at the walls, scarlet creepers*
> *endlessly growing.'*

What on earth was that all about? He turned the pages, and other lines caught his eye:

> *'Think of her as a bird: pull her white wings*
> *as wide as they'll go before the feathers separate.*
> *Think of her as a tree: leave her to shed herself*
> *at the proper time. Think of her as ice:*
> *put her by the kitchen stove to disappear.'*

Blimey, Laurie thought. What *was* she getting at? He quite liked enigmatic poems, but had never dared admit to anyone his feeling that if something didn't have a decent rhyme scheme or at the very least a driving rhythm, it wasn't *really, truly* poetry, but more like prose cut up and dotted about the page in short chunkettes. When he got back to school, he'd show the book to his English teacher and see what he thought of it.

Still, imagine Carrie writing all that stuff! Did she really think of herself as a bird, or a lump of ice? Maybe she did. Why not? He himself, after a practically sleepless night, felt like nothing so much as . . . what? A soggy dishcloth. A plate of porridge. Any drippy, messy sort of thing would do. He felt as though he'd never be solid and upright again and wished for the thousandth time that Irene had a TV. A mindless Christmas movie might have cheered him up.

11.30 a.m. The Pink Room

'OK, Mother,' said Laurie. 'Give. What's all the secrecy about?'

'Sit down, dear,' Letta said. 'There's something I have to tell you.'

'Ooh,' Laurie said. 'How frightfully thrilling! Whatever can it be? And why have we been chosen to hear this revelation? What about Dad?'

'Dad knows already. And I wish you wouldn't be so flippant, Laurie. Take something seriously for once.'

'The joke on my lips is not an indicator of how I feel. Far from it! If you want to know,' he said, and smiled at Marianne, 'my heart is *broken*.'

'Oh, shut up, Laurie, and come and sit down,' Marianne said.

They spread themselves out on the bed, and Letta, who was sitting on the armchair, got up and went to stand by the window.

'I think it's getting warmer,' she said. 'I do really. This morning, I thought I heard a sort of dripping, like icicles melting.' She turned to face her children. 'It's very hard to know where to begin. It always looks so easy in plays on the TV and on stage. I wish I had a script . . .'

'You haven't,' said Marianne curtly, 'so get on with it.'

'Yes,' said Letta. 'I will. I've met someone.'

Her children stared at her and said nothing. She went on: 'I've fallen in love with him.'

Still silence, and four eyes looking at her.

'I've asked your father for a divorce. Robert . . . that's his name . . . and I plan to be married as soon as the divorce comes through.'

Marianne jumped off the bed, and said: 'I told Ellie I thought you were having an affair, but I didn't think for a minute that it was *true*. God, Mum, that's . . . it's disgusting. It's perfectly obvious you don't care about Dad or Laurie or me, so I've got some news of my own to tell you. I don't see why I have to go pussyfooting around any longer trying to spare *your* feelings. You're going to do exactly what you want with your life, and so am I. And don't think you can stop me.'

'Marianne, wait . . . you're not making any sense at all. Don't you want to know more? Details? More about Robert?'

Marianne made a vomiting noise in her throat, and flung herself back on the bed, face down.

'No, Mum,' Laurie said quietly. 'We don't want to know *anything*. Not about your bloke . . . I refuse to say his name . . . not about how you met him or how overwhelming your passion is for one another . . . nothing. Not one thing.'

'Why are you both being so . . . harsh?' Letta's voice was full of tears. 'Hasn't either one of you ever . . . well, never mind . . . haven't you got any *feelings*?'

Marianne turned round, her face red, and her eyes blazing.

'I've got feelings. I feel sad for Dad. And for us. I feel . . . unloved by my own mother. I feel furious. And you're so selfish that you never even heard what I said before. I'm not *ever* going to consider your point of view ever again. I'm leaving school after the exams next summer and going to Drama School, and you can stuff your A levels and universities, so there!'

'I'm not going to be sidetracked,' said Letta, 'by your childish blackmailing. As far as I'm concerned, I'm still your mother and till you're eighteen you'll do exactly as your father and I decide.'

'I shan't,' said Marianne. 'I shall do exactly what *I* want, and you won't be able to stop me.'

'This is', said Letta, 'irrelevant for the moment. We have to make major decisions about our lives, all of us, but all I wanted to do now was tell you . . . tell you how I feel.'

'It's OK, Mum,' said Laurie. 'We know, both of us, exactly how you feel. Now do you mind leaving us alone?'

'Isn't there anything you want to ask me?'

'No,' said Laurie. 'What you've told us is distressing, but hardly difficult. We both understand everything perfectly. Have you told Irene?'

'No,' said Letta. 'I thought I'd leave it—'

'Coward!' Marianne shouted. 'You're a coward, and you don't love us, so don't say you do!'

Letta left the room in tears.

'Look what you've done now, sister dear,' Laurie said.

'Good,' said Marianne. 'I'm glad. She deserves it. I'm not a bit sorry for her.'

1.00 p.m. The Attic

Marianne hardly ever cried and when she did, she made sure that no one could see her doing it. It was such a revolting process . . . leaking all that water and making your nose run and your eyes sore was quite bad enough without the added disgrace of everyone seeing you looking puffy and red and *ugly*. She hated, also, not being in control of herself; having her emotions flung about every which way. And until she knew that she could appear normal, it was far better to hide away. She sat on the floor next to the costume trunk and tried to think back to when she was little and used to spend hours and hours up here, pretending to be a lady in Irene's opera gowns.

When the first storm of weeping had passed, she wiped

her nose with an ancient tissue from the back pocket of her jeans. She was beginning to calm down and making an effort to breathe more evenly, when Ellie's head appeared at the top of the ladder, closely followed by the rest of her.

'Marianne,' she said. 'Here you are. Have you been crying? What's happened? Oh, Marianne . . .'

Marianne looked at her cousin. Part of her, she could feel it, wanted to shout at her: get lost, go away, never come back, and don't dare tell anyone where I am. But the look on Ellie's face, of love and concern and *caring*, made her instead burst into new tears, and say: 'Ellie . . . oh, Ellie, what's going to happen to us?'

Ellie didn't bother to answer, but ran to Marianne and hugged her hard and for a long time. She stroked her, and murmured quietly without actually saying anything. Gradually, Marianne's crying stopped.

'Tell me,' Ellie said.

'There's nothing to tell. And you're probably the last person to tell it to. It's no different, really, from what's already happened to you. I feel boring just saying the words . . . they're so *ordinary*. My parents are getting divorced. There.'

'Letta and Derek? I don't believe it. They've been married for ages . . .'

'Well, so what? Your mum and dad had as well. It makes no difference. The dreaded Love can evidently strike you any time, anywhere, however old and respectable and married you are. Letta has met the love of her life and has to be with him, even though it means leaving us. I don't care. Let her go. I don't need a mother any more. I'm going to be sixteen next year, and that's practically grown up.'

'I know,' Ellie said, 'but you can't help feeling that you're sort of second-best when they don't want to stay with you. They wouldn't like it if the boot were on the other foot. Imagine if kids decided they'd had enough of their parents and left them for another family altogether. They'd soon put a stop to that.'

'I'll get over it. You seem to be all right most of the time. So do all my friends at school. There's hardly a person I know who isn't in the same situation.'

Ellie nodded. 'It *does* get better, after a bit,' she said, 'but I still feel sad sometimes. I was going to phone him yesterday and then I couldn't, and that's awful . . . I feel so far away from him. Do you think he'd ever forget about me? Letta would never forget about you.'

'Of course he never would. You have,' said Marianne, 'a very romantic view of mothers. Look at whatever-her-name-is . . . Serena . . . and Olivia. She didn't hang around very long, did she?'

'But Letta . . .' Ellie said. 'She loves you. You know she does. And Derek loves you. And you've got Laurie. He adores you.'

'They're in an even worse state than me. Poor old Dad! He's known for ages. He's only kept quiet for our sake . . . mine and Laurie's.' Marianne clambered to her feet.

'Come on, Ellie,' she said. 'Let's go down. I'm fed up with mooching about. Stuff the lot of them, that's what I say. After next summer, I shall be off to Drama School and no one will see me for dust.'

'What about me, Marianne? Can't I see you? Or write to you, wherever you are? *You* aren't going to disappear as well, are you? I couldn't bear that.'

Ellie looked so crestfallen that Marianne laughed.

'Of course not, silly! You're like my little sister. I'll always stay in touch with you.'

Ellie smiled and followed her cousin downstairs.

'Do I look OK?' Marianne said. 'I must go and wash my face.'

'You look fine,' said Ellie. 'Absolutely normal.'

'I suppose I feel more normal now. Except that I could cheerfully *strangle* my mother.'

'Maybe she couldn't help it,' Ellie said. 'Like you said: love just *hit* her. Sort of swept her away.'

Marianne laughed. 'I wasn't being serious. What *have* you been reading? Do you believe that sort of rubbish?'

'I don't know,' said Ellie. 'I think I do.'

'Well, I don't,' said Marianne. 'That's for things like the movies . . . or the opera. Not for real life.'

3.00 p.m. The Basement Flat

In the few months that she had been feeling poorly, Nana had never dared to say it. But now she felt braver. She looked in the mirror and spoke the word aloud for the first time: 'Cancer.'

There, that wasn't so bad. She had lived with the idea of it for so long that it had almost stopped being terrifying. She said it again, more firmly. She would be optimistic. Mind over matter . . . she was a great believer in that.

I might have years and years more to live, she thought. Already I'm way beyond the threescore years and ten the Bible tells us we can have. She had decided, also, to stop fretting about the appointment. There was nothing she could do about it. Dr Holden would realize that the weather was to blame for her not keeping the appointment and not phoning to explain. Perhaps *his* telephone wasn't working either. Perhaps the whole country was in the grip of winter, and no one could go anywhere. She would get in touch when the thaw came and that was that.

After that bad turn just before Christmas dinner, she had managed to keep the pain away most of the time. And now that it was over, well, she didn't really care what happened. The main work of cooking and preparation was done with for this year. And even if everyone had to stay another week, there was enough in the freezers. No one would starve. If only Pamina would come back, Nana thought, I wouldn't have much to complain about. It's all gone better than I expected.

4.45 p.m. The Lake

'Marianne! Wait! Wait for me!' Carlo followed the dark shape running through the snow towards the Lake. 'Where are you going?'

The shape stood still and turned towards him. She was dressed in her puffy anorak and boots, and her face was white against the dark material of her hood.

'Not far enough, thanks to this...' She bent down, picked up a handful of snow and began to knead it. 'If it wasn't for this weather, I'd be out of here. I'd be down that road and on a train and away... I can't bear it. I just can't stand it. The whole thing. Everything. It's... oh, I don't know.'

'Stop,' Carlo said. 'Calm down. They're all shell-shocked in there. No one's saying anything. What did you do to them?'

'I told my mother that I was leaving school next July and going to Drama School. Laurie's known for ages. She's the one who's told everyone else and made them all hysterical. Why do they care so much? It's my life . . . it's my career. Why should I stay at school any longer than I need to? My mother deserves everything she gets, anyway. Don't you think she does? Have you heard about what's happened from Laurie?'

'No,' said Carlo. 'I've been helping Ellie look for Pamina again.'

'Oh, my,' said Marianne. 'All sorts of unmentionable stuff has been hitting the fan. My mother is behaving like something from a very silly novel. She's in *lurve*. Have you ever heard anything so revolting? I feel sick when I think about it.'

Carlo was silent. 'You shouldn't say that. I don't think there's anything revolting about love.'

'But she's so old! And what's Dad supposed to do? And what about us? We're her children, for God's sake. She's going to leave us. She's going to take our life and shake it and turn it upside down. She's got to have what *she* wants . . . always. Doesn't matter about the rest of us. You've seen Dad. He looks awful: grey and pinched. And Laurie, well, let's just say I don't think this Christmas is going to be among his Top Ten Favourite Times, thanks to you and Mum.'

'Me?' Carlo looked aghast. 'What have I done?'

'Nothing,' said Marianne. 'Forget I ever said anything. Honestly, I didn't mean to. Laurie will kill me.

'You can't, Marianne. Not now you've said that . . . what am I supposed to have done?'

'Promise me,' Marianne whispered. 'Promise me you won't say a word to him.'

'Of course I won't.'

'He's . . . well, he's jealous of us.' Carlo was silent, waiting for more. Marianne continued. 'You must have realized that he was very fond of you.'

'I like him too,' said Carlo. 'He's my friend.'

Marianne kicked the snow, suddenly irritated.

'Do you need pictures drawn for you or something? Laurie loves you. He's in love with you. And if you ever tell him I told you, I'll never even *look* at you ever again.'

They walked towards the Lake without speaking, and stood beside the frozen water in the dark.

'I think I knew,' Carlo said slowly. 'I don't feel surprised, so maybe I've known for a long time, at some level. He even said he had something to tell me, yesterday. Maybe he's thought better of it.' He sighed. 'I won't say anything. I promise.'

He took her hand. 'Come back to the house now, Marianne. It's freezing.'

'You're not properly dressed.'

'I raced out after you.'

'More fool you,' said Marianne. She began to stride up the hill, towards the Golden House.

Carlo shouted: 'Marianne!' But she raced ahead and he had to run after her, his feet dragged down by the snow. She stopped and waited for him beside the Snow Lady.

'Is it my imagination,' she asked, 'or is this creature sort of slithering downwards? Could she possibly be thawing? Or is that wishful thinking?'

Carlo didn't answer. Instead, he unfastened the silver

cloak and removed it from the Snow Lady's white shoulders. He came close to Marianne and threw it around her, kissing her as he did up the clasp.

'Come inside,' he said. 'The only bit of me that I can feel is my mouth.'

They turned to walk into the house. Just before they opened the door, Marianne looked back at the icy figure on the lawn.

'What's that?' she said.

'Where?'

'There . . . just where the Lady's skirt meets the ground . . . a sort of lump.'

'Wait here,' said Carlo. 'I'll go and see.'

'I'm coming too,' said Marianne.

They found Pamina's body curled into a sleeping shape. Carlo took the silver cloak from around Marianne's shoulders, and wrapped the old cat tenderly up in its glittering folds. Marianne felt the tears prick again in her eyes and, before she could stop herself, she began to weep. Twice in one day, after years and years of being so cool. But death was not like anything else. Poor Pamina! Some of the tears were for her, but not all of them.

Work Rota: Laurie and Derek

'I believe,' said Derek, 'that this is what they call an aftermath.'

Laurie was uncharacteristically quiet, cutting up vegetables at the kitchen table ('just anything that happens to be around, really,') for Nana's Winter Salad, and looking steadily at the knife. He was trying very hard to keep himself under control, because he felt that once his mouth were to

134

open, all sorts of things might pop out ... weeping and wailing and gnashing of teeth were the very least of it. He nodded, just to show Derek that he was listening.

'She's told you and Marianne, I gather,' Derek went on. 'It's best to talk about it, you know. Doesn't do to go bottling everything up.'

Laurie laughed. 'That's rich coming from you! Mister Let-it-all-hang-out himself.'

'Maybe I should have,' Derek murmured. 'Perhaps things would have worked out differently if only I'd been a different sort of chap. You never know.'

'Oh yes, I do!' Laurie turned to face his father. 'Don't you start being guilty about something that's entirely Mum's fault.'

'I don't think these things are ever anybody's fault. Not really.'

'Of course they are. And it's not yours, so stop being all pathetic. We'll manage very well on our own.'

'You children don't have to manage. Your mother *is* still your mother, and will want to see as much of you as she possibly can.'

'She can forget it,' Laurie said, between clenched teeth. 'I'm not spending a day under the same roof as Lover Boy.' He chopped viciously into a radish, then flung the knife across the table and put his head between his hands and began to sob.

'Laurie?' Derek was immediately beside him. 'What's the matter, old chap? Are you crying?'

'Yes,' Laurie said, sniffing. 'Isn't it pathetic? Do you know how many years it is since I did this? I've lost count. I didn't think I *could* any more. I thought I'd forgotten.'

135

'Oh, you never forget,' said Derek. 'However old and crusty you get. But don't cry. You've got so much to look forward to . . .'

'Really? At the moment, I can't think of a single thing.' He wiped his tears away with the backs of his hands and sniffed. 'I'm going to say something, Dad, and I'm going to do it quickly because it's hard. I'm gay. I asked Carlo to stay because . . . well, because I liked him, only I think he likes Marianne. This Christmas has been a disaster. And we can't even go home—'

'Stop,' said Derek. 'Stop talking for a second. You're filling the air, that's all. Putting up a kind of smokescreen, but I heard it. You're gay, you said. Are you sure? I mean, you're very young—'

'And it's just a phase I'm going through, right? Just wait till I meet the girl of my dreams, et cetera, et cetera. Do me a favour, Dad. I'm seventeen. I've known how I feel about stuff like this for years. Years and years. Are you going to banish me? Never speak to me again?'

'Don't be childish, Laurie.'

'I'm not being childish. I can see you're not happy about it.'

Derek smiled. 'I can't pretend I'm thrilled to bits, it's true but—'

'Why not?' Laurie cried. 'Why don't you just want me to be happy?'

'I *do*,' Derek said. 'I *do* just want you to be happy, and that's why I'm a bit, well, apprehensive. Being gay doesn't make life easier, you know. You're going to meet prejudice for one thing.'

'Tell me about it,' Laurie muttered.

'Not from me,' Derek said quickly. 'You know you won't get prejudice from me. But I *will* worry, Laurie. I won't be able to help it. You'll be careful, won't you?'

'Yes, Dad,' said Laurie. 'I promise.'

Derek looked at his son and felt ashamed, because something that felt exactly like sorrow had filled his heart, in spite of all his brave words.

At that moment, the kitchen door opened and Marianne and Carlo came in with something wrapped up in what looked like silver foil.

'Oh, Dad,' Marianne said. 'Laurie, look. It's Pamina. She's dead.'

Derek took the bundle from her arms and she fell weeping into a chair.

'Everything's *AWFUL*!' she sobbed. 'I want to go home.'

9.30 p.m. The Dining Room

Carlo couldn't get over the family's reaction to Pamina's death. OK, she was a much-loved pet, and OK she'd been part of the family for longer than any of the children but, still, she *was* just a cat, and they shouldn't have been that surprised. Most cats don't live till the age of twenty. Around his streets, they were lucky not to be squashed under passing cars when they were no more than kittens.

Wisely, he kept his thoughts to himself, and got even further into Marianne's good books (he hoped) by helping to carry the creature out to the gazebo, where she was going to lie (all wrapped in her special blanket, and laid in a box) till the ground was soft enough to dig. She was going to be buried under her favourite camellia bush. Honestly! Carlo tucked into his spaghetti, and kept quiet. That Ellie was soppy he could understand, but Marianne and Laurie and most of the adults too, looked to him in the terminal stages of doom and gloom, in spite of all the comforting words that Edmund produced. He must, Carlo thought, be used to cheering people up after their pets had died.

To be fair, though, maybe it wasn't *all* to do with Pamina. Laurie . . . well, Carlo thought, his long face is probably down to me, and Marianne is upset about her parents' divorce, however tough she talks. Ellie's got her mother's abortion, Edmund most likely doesn't know what to do about his kid now that her mother's done a bunk, and Irene looks as though she's about to go to the guillotine or something. As Carlo was thinking about her, she fingered the pearls that circled her throat and began to speak.

'Everyone, I'd like to say something, if that's all right. I know that we are all feeling sad about Pamina, but she had a long and a very happy life, and I know that she, for one, would be glad *not* to be here for what I'm about to tell you.'

She paused dramatically and looked all round the table. Talk about getting people's attention, thought Laurie.

'I wanted you all to have a wonderful Christmas this year,' she said. And from everyone came little murmurs about how wonderful Christmas had been, and how lovely everything was. Irene moved her hand slightly, and silence fell again.

She continued: 'It was important to me that everything be perfect, because this is the last Christmas we shall be spending in this house. And before you all begin to shout at me, let me explain. Running the Golden House has become too much for me. I am, after all, not as young as I was.' She paused to allow some time for those who wished to contradict her, but everyone was listening too intently to be gallant.

'I have sold the Golden House to a chain of hotels,' she continued. 'I have received a very good price for it, and I've bought a flat in London for myself and Nana and Frederick . . . I will be able to afford a nurse for the Maestro . . . it's getting a little too much for Nana and Carrie.'

'It's not,' said Carrie. 'It's not too much at all. And what about me? Where will I go? This is my home. I can't . . .' Carrie bent her head, her eyes full of tears. 'I couldn't live in London.'

'I have put a deposit down,' said Irene calmly, 'on one of the houses in the village.'

'May I say something, please?' Edmund actually stood up to speak.

'Certainly,' said Irene.

He looked at Carrie, then down at the floor.

'This isn't how I wished to say it,' he began. 'I had meant it to come after an appropriate period of courtship, and I had meant to address Carrie alone. Still, circumstances dictate—'

'Yes?' Irene was clearly growing impatient. Someone else, Laurie thought, is in the limelight.

'I intend to ask Carrie to be my wife,' he said, and cheers broke out. Carrie blushed, and hid her face in her hands. 'After my divorce comes through, naturally.'

He turned to Carrie. She nodded at him, and more exclamations of delight rose round the table.

'That solves that problem,' Laurie muttered to Carlo.

'Carrie exchanges one Gothic Pile for another. The Gables is just an ugly version of this place. She'll be in heaven. Love conquers all.'

Marianne suddenly pushed her chair aside and stood up. Her face was scarlet, and Laurie could see that she was making an enormous effort not to cry.

'Irene, how *could* you?' she said. 'I can't believe you'd sell the Golden House without telling anyone . . . without talking about it. I think it's cruel. I think you're wicked, *wicked* to do such a thing. You obviously don't care about us. We all thought the Golden House was . . . well, like our house, and that it would always be here for us, and now . . . oh, I can't bear it. Everything's changing. I hate it . . .'

She ran out of the room.

'Go after her, Laurence dear, and calm her down. She will soon,' Irene said, 'realize that I did what I thought was right for all of us.'

But most of all, Laurie thought, you did what was right for *you*. You always do. Later, he would tell Marianne how spooky it had been to hear Irene echo his very thought.

She looked straight at him and said: 'Of course, most of all, I did what was right for me. I always do.'

'We are leaving?' The Maestro was beginning to understand. 'Perhaps we will be going to Paris?'

'No, Maestro,' said Nana, taking his hand and patting it. 'We are going to London.'

'Covent Garden,' said the Maestro longingly. 'We will be going to the Opera?'

'Of course,' said Irene. 'We will go to everything.'

The Maestro nodded, satisfied.

140

10.00 p.m. The White Room

Carrie was sitting in an armchair, nursing little Olivia. Edmund stood at the window, looking out at the garden.

'I will miss her,' she said, 'when you go back to The Gables. Isn't it strange? I've never thought of myself as a maternal person.'

'You are kind,' said Edmund. 'A small, helpless creature makes you maternal. And of course, when we marry, she will be your child as well. Carrie . . .'

'Yes?'

'Will you miss the Golden House? Will you be able to live with me at The Gables?'

Carrie wanted to say: I would live with you anywhere, but she simply answered: 'Yes, of course.'

'It's an old and fusty place. We will have to make it more . . . habitable.'

'And we will,' said Carrie. No one knew, and Irene never acknowledged, that it was *she* who had been overseeing the Golden House decor, ever since she could remember. She had kept quiet, partly because it was her habit, and also because Irene, after all, was famous for her wonderful taste. Now she, Carrie, would make Edmund's house beautiful.

'Will you mind having them all to stay for Christmas? I'd like to continue the traditions . . .'

'Nothing,' said Edmund, 'would give me greater pleasure.' He was not exaggerating. At this moment, with his daughter sleeping in Carrie's arms, he considered himself truly blessed. The divorce, and its attendant problems, he would put aside till the New Year.

11.00 p.m. The Pink Room

Laurie and Carlo sat on the armchairs in Marianne's room, discussing Irene's astonishing news. Marianne and Ellie were both sitting on the bed, leaning against the headboard. Ellie had been crying.

'I'm sorry,' she said, 'but I think it's awful. We'll never have a proper Christmas again. No Golden House, and no Pamina . . .' Her voice trailed away. She could have gone on . . . and no proper father, and no baby sister, and a sad mother. She felt very sorry for herself.

'And it's not as if *we* can do a proper Christmas in our house,' said Laurie. 'Thanks to our beloved parents deciding to split up . . . perfect timing as usual.'

They sat in silence, then Marianne said: 'I know. We'll work on Carrie and Edmund. I'm sure they'll ask us all down to their house.'

'It won't be the same,' said Laurie. 'The Gables is a chilly sort of place.'

'But it *has* got a television,' said Ellie. Everyone smiled. 'I'm sure we can still have a good time.'

'*If* we can persuade Carrie . . .' said Laurie.

'We will,' said Ellie. 'I'm sure we will. She loves the Christmas stuff as much as we do, doesn't she?'

'Yes,' said Laurie. 'She's even written a poem about it. I can't remember exactly what she says, but basically it's pro-Christmas.'

'Find it,' said Marianne. She picked up Carrie's book and tossed it at her brother.

He leafed through the pages for a few moments, and then said: 'Here it is, look, I'll read you what she says:

' "When the curtains are drawn, the yellow light
shines on what we remember of childhood:
a tree prettily transformed, and sweets
left where we can find them; snow if we're lucky,
and a mother's voice singing.
Binding threads of gold." '

Ellie said: 'Are you sure that's about Christmas?'

'Of course it is,' said Laurie. 'All that stuff about trees and snow. I didn't realize Carrie was so sentimental.'

'I think it's lovely,' said Ellie.

'It's *awful*,' said Laurie. 'Mawkish and ... and ... well, gooey.'

'Christmas is gooey,' said Ellie, and they laughed.

Marianne froze.

'Can you hear something? Listen. It's the phone! It's working again. Alleluia!'

She jumped off the bed and raced for the door. The others followed her downstairs.

27 DECEMBER

Menus for the Day

LUNCH
Green-pepper soup
Cracked-wheat salad
Garlic bread

HIGH TEA
Omelettes
Chickpea salad
Mince pies

Under the snow, the grass had been waiting, and now patches of it were appearing all over the lawn. The weight of white on the trees was sliding from the branches to the ground, and telephone lines hummed with conversations that should have taken place days ago. Everything was returning to normal.

12.00 a.m. The Garret Room

Frederick looked out of the window. His head was suddenly very clear. Irene had sold the Golden House. They would be moving. Would everything he had collected fit into his cases? Where were his cases? How would they travel? Perhaps it would be by train. He had always loved trains and, although he hadn't been anywhere for years, he still recalled the sound of their whistles, the smell of their steam. How lovely it would be to sit in a theatre again. There was nowhere, nowhere in the world as beautiful and full of *adventures* as a theatre. But Carrie . . . she was staying here, somehow. He had not quite understood why, but one thing was certain. She was not coming to town. But she would visit. She had said she would, and Carrie always kept her word.

'My little girl,' he muttered to himself, and then shook his head. No, that wasn't right. Irene was married to Ivor. The girls were *his* girls, except for Carrie. Was that right? *Is* that what Irene had told him, years ago? He couldn't escape the feeling that his head was growing more and more foggy and fuzzy. Perhaps he was muddled. The clear times were growing shorter and shorter. But he felt differently about Carrie. He was sure of that.

12.30 a.m. The Blue Room

'Ellie, are you asleep?'

'No, Mum, of course not. I'm much too excited to sleep. Wasn't it wonderful, speaking to Dad on the phone? And he'd been trying and trying to get through. Come and sit on the bed. Could you ever in your life imagine such a great Christmas present? I couldn't. It's the best thing ever . . . and it wasn't Dad's fault that he didn't tell me before Christmas . . . it *was* all that snow, after all. But I don't care. It's even better coming now, when I need cheering up.'

'Ellie, that's what I've come to talk to you about. Are you feeling a little . . . well, a little more . . . forgiving towards me?'

Ellie flung her arms round Susanna's neck. 'Oh, Mum,

I'm so sorry. I should have thought . . . are you upset? I mean, Cynthia is going to have a baby, and you . . . well . . .'

'It's all right, really. A baby is the last thing I need, truly. But I know how much you wanted a sister or brother, and if your father and Cynthia can provide you with one, that's great.'

'You're not jealous?'

'No,' said Susanna. 'And what's more, I'm delighted that he's asked you over to the States for *next* Christmas . . . the baby will be over four months old by then, and you'll have the time of your life. It will almost make up for not being in the Golden House.'

Ellie sighed.

'What about Marianne and Laurie? We were going to work on Carrie to have all of us at the Gables.'

Susanna laughed. 'Honestly, Ellie, you're never happy . . . you can have Christmas there another year. Or not. Why do you worry so much?'

'I can't help it,' Ellie said. 'I just do. And, Mum?'

'Yes?'

'About the abortion. I do understand. Really I do. I'm sorry I behaved so badly, when you were feeling rotten.'

'That's OK,' said Susanna. 'Go to sleep now, love. We'll maybe be leaving tomorrow night, if this thaw continues.'

'Is there a thaw?' Ellie asked. 'Will the snow be gone by morning?'

'Not gone, no,' said Susanna. 'But going. Shrinking all the time.'

After her mother left the room, Ellie lay in the dark, thinking about her new American sister . . . or brother. Then she remembered the Snow Lady, and jumped out of bed.

146

She ran to the window and looked out. There she was, by the gazebo, and she had definitely shrunk. She was no more than a few small lumps sticking out of the lawn now. By tomorrow there wouldn't be much left of her at all.

10.30 a.m. The Brown Room

'Laurie?'

Laurie stopped putting things into his case, and turned to face Carlo.

'I just wanted to thank you. I've never had a Christmas like this. I love the Golden House. I can really understand you and Marianne being so upset about leaving it. I feel as if . . . I don't know.'

'As if you're being exiled from Paradise?'

'Right. And I shall always, always remember it.'

'That's OK. I've had a good time too.'

'Is that true?' Carlo asked.

'Sure. It's been brilliant.'

He laid his pyjamas on top of all his other clothes, and turned away from Carlo. He couldn't do it. He wasn't going to be able to say the words. What if Carlo knew already? What if he guessed? Then let *him* say something. Laurie hated himself. There won't be a better chance, said a voice in his head. Speak, dammit. But he knew he would never take the risk. Carlo might be disgusted. What if, thought Laurie, what if he no longer wants to be my friend? That didn't bear thinking about. Best not to rock the boat. But say something now, to break the silence . . . anything.

He said: 'I'm a bit sad though. I'll miss this place.'

'Me too,' said Carlo. 'And what about Marianne? I was amazed at her reaction. I didn't think she rated the Golden

House much. Shows how much I know. I'm going to find her. She spoke to that Andy earlier on. She's probably ready to finish with me.'

'I'm sure she isn't,' said Laurie, and waved at Carlo as he left the room.

When he was alone, Laurie looked at his reflection in the mirror, and wiped away the tears that had suddenly filled his eyes and were threatening to fall. He zipped up his case, and left the room.

11.00 a.m. The Pink Room

'Marianne? Are you busy? May I come in?'

'Yes, come on, Carlo. You can help me sit on my case. I pack too many things, every year. I never learn. I never wear half the things I bring. I'm stupid.' She smiled at him.

'You look happier. Are you?'

'Much better. I don't know what all that was about, before. I suppose it was the shock. I usually can't wait for Christmas to be over, but never being able to come here again . . . well, it's hard to take in. Anyway, I'm OK now. I *want* to get home, in fact.'

'That's because of Andy, right?'

Marianne flashed him a radiant smile. 'Right.'

She paused and looked at Carlo more closely. 'You're frowning, Carlo. You wouldn't be jealous by any chance?'

'Go to the top of the class,' said Carlo. 'Of course I am. I thought . . . well, I thought we had . . . I mean, I thought you knew . . .'

'Knew what? That you fancied me? I knew all right. And I like you a lot. Don't think I don't.'

'I helped to pass the time. That's what you're saying.'

'I am *not*,' said Marianne. 'Give me credit for a bit of feeling.'

She blushed as she said this, knowing that he wasn't a hundred per cent wrong.

'I really *do* like you,' she said again.

'But you like this Andy person better.'

Marianne didn't answer at first. Then she said: 'I'm going to a New Year's Eve Party with him. I'm sorry.'

She took a step towards Carlo, thinking to kiss him . . . to kiss him goodbye, but he side-stepped her and opened the door.

'Don't give it another thought,' said Carlo, and left the room. I'm *not* going to let her see that she's got to me, he thought, as he walked down the corridor. I'm glad I never told her I loved her. He felt desolate, as though someone had stripped his heart of everything and left it looking like a white room cleared of every piece of furniture and every picture.

4.45 p.m. The Front Hall

Irene, Nana, Carrie and the Maestro stood on the doorstep and waved, as the cars made their way down the drive to the gate. The Springers and Carlo were in one car, and Susanna and Ellie in the other. The roads, Derek had ascertained from the RAC, were passable, if a little perilous still. When the last tail light had disappeared from view, Irene turned and went inside and the others followed her. She sighed and recognized in the sigh something of relief.

'There,' she said. 'It's over. How sad, the very last Christmas in this house.'

Nana hurried to the kitchen with Carrie to put together something for supper.

The Maestro wandered into the Library, wondering where the cat had got to. It seemed to him that he hadn't seen her for a long time. Irene went into the Chinese Lounge. The tree was still hung about with coloured ribbons.

'Tomorrow,' Irene said to herself. 'I will deal with you tomorrow. Have one more night of being beautiful.'

And Pamina . . . Edmund had promised to dig her a grave, under the camellia. Perhaps, she thought, I will get a kitten when we move. She began to turn over in her mind suitable names for the new cat.